Praise for Elin Hilderbrand's
WINTER STREET

"Open this diverting tale of family dysfunction and you'll find a holiday package filled with humor, romance, and realism."
—Jocelyn McClurg, *USA Today*

"This charming holiday novel—hilarious and slightly gut-wrenching at the same time—is a treat that can be enjoyed year-round—even during the hottest summer months. Readers will connect with at least one of the Quinn family members and appreciate the happy reunion of this very dysfunctional yet accepting family."
—Sarah Eisenbraun, RT Book Reviews.com

"The holidays wouldn't be complete without a little family dysfunction, and Hilderbrand writes it well."
—Melissa DeWild, *Library Journal*

"A frothy tale."   —*Booklist*

"*Winter Street* is a hilarious page-turner. Never one to disappoint her readers, Hilderbrand has produced yet another classic novel."   —Vivian Payton, BookReporter.com

ALSO BY ELIN HILDERBRAND

The Beach Club

Nantucket Nights

Summer People

The Blue Bistro

The Love Season

Barefoot

A Summer Affair

The Castaways

The Island

Silver Girl

Summerland

Beautiful Day

The Matchmaker

The Rumor

Winter Stroll

WINTER STREET

A NOVEL

Elin Hilderbrand

BACK BAY BOOKS

Little, Brown and Company

New York Boston London

Copyright © 2014 by Elin Hilderbrand
Excerpt from *Winter Stroll* copyright © 2015 by Elin Hilderbrand
Reading group guide copyright © 2015 Elin Hilderbrand and
Little, Brown and Company

Back Bay Books / Little, Brown and Company
Hachette Book Group
1290 Avenue of the Americas, New York, NY 10104
littlebrown.com

Originally published in hardcover by Little, Brown and Company, October 2014
First Back Bay paperback edition, October 2015

Back Bay Books is an imprint of Little, Brown and Company. The Back Bay Books name and logo are trademarks of Hachette Book Group, Inc.

The publisher is not responsible for websites (or their content) that are not owned by the publisher.

The Hachette Speakers Bureau provides a wide range of authors for speaking events. To find out more, go to hachettespeakersbureau.com or call (866) 376-6591.

ISBN 978-0-316-37611-2 (hc) / 978-0-316-41066-3 (large print) / 978-0-316-37610-5 (pb) / 978-0-316-34124-0 (signed edition)
Library of Congress Control Number: 2014940628

10 9 8 7 6 5 4 3 2 1

RRD-C

Printed in the United States of America

For Judith and Duane Thurman,
who have kept my paper angel ornament,
as well as all of my other childhood memories,
cherished and safe these many years.
Hugs and love.

DECEMBER 23

KELLEY

He thinks nothing of walking into room 10 without knocking. The door is unlocked, and George hasn't checked in yet, anyway. George is due on the eleven-thirty ferry with his 1931 Model A fire engine, a bespoke Santa Claus vehicle, but he was delayed because of snow in the western part of the state. George has gamely brought the fire engine over and donned the red suit every December for the past twelve years. George weighs in at 305 pounds, give or take the five, and is the jolly owner of a full head of white hair and a white goatee (new since his divorce; before, it was a full beard). Kelley wants George to arrive so that Mitzi will relax. According to Mitzi, no one can possibly replace George, and nothing ruins Christmas like an absent Santa.

When Kelley swings open the door to room 10, he realizes he's intruding. There are two people in the room, kissing. Kelley's first instinct — the instinct of everyone he knows when walking in on something private — is to blurt out

"Sorry!" and slam the door shut. (He has a quick, unfortunate vision of his aunt Cissy on the toilet during his grandfather's wake.) But what he just caught the shortest glimpse of, the length of one frame of film, was nothing like his aunt Cissy on the john. It was two people in full, passionate lip lock—"necking," they used to call it in high school. The click of the door instantly reveals the identity of those people.

It's George, their Santa Claus, and Mitzi, Kelley's wife.

Kelley flings the door back open, fast enough that George and Mitzi have yet to fully disengage. George still has his hands on Mitzi's hips, and Mitzi's hands are buried in George's white hair.

"What...?" Kelley says. He's not sure what to think. He has been in crisis for weeks. First of all, it's December, a month he used to own on Nantucket. He had a full inn through Thanksgiving and Christmas Stroll, but he hasn't had a paying guest since the tenth of December. Normally, he has a waiting list during the week of Christmas (just like the original Christmas: no room at the inn). The Drellwiches and the Kasperzacks used to come to see their grandchildren, the Elmers came to escape their grandchildren, and the other four rooms were taken by young couples who found Nantucket a charming place to spend the holiday— and then, of course, there was always George. But this year, nobody. This year, the neon sign in Kelley's mind flashes. VACANCY, VACANCY! It's his least favorite word in the English language, especially since his finances are in such precarious shape. Kelley has kept the inn up and running for nineteen years by supplementing the inn's budget with the treasure trove of savings he had when he left his "real" job, trading petroleum futures in New York. That treasure trove has now dwindled to an amount in the high four figures. Lately, Kelley has fantasized about selling the inn off as a private home—it would fetch between four and five million, he guesses—and moving to Hawaii. His ex-wife, Margaret, is flying to Maui on Christmas Eve, as soon as she finishes anchoring the CBS *Evening News.* When she told Kelley this a few weeks ago, he felt a category 5 pang of jealousy. He thought, *Please take me with you.*

But the deeper reason Kelley has been addled is because his youngest son, Bart—who had been stationed in Vilseck, Germany, for two months, where it was all "pretzels and blondes"—was deployed to Sangin, Afghanistan, on December 19. He sent Kelley and Mitzi a text that said, *Made it in country. Love you.* And that was the last they heard. The texts that Kelley and Mitzi tried to send back were "undeliverable." Kelley's e-mails go through, but they remain unanswered. Kelley imagines his words whipping across sandy, inhospitable terrain.

Bart is the only child Kelley fathered with Mitzi, and he has been raised as a bit of a golden boy—favored, pampered, spoiled—or so the other three Quinn children would claim. Kelley thought the Marines would be the best choice for Bart, but now that he's gone, Kelley is racked with anxiety. And his anxiety is nothing compared with Mitzi's. Mitzi has been a basket case.

Although she doesn't appear to be worrying about Bart at the moment.

"Kelley," she says, while tucking in her shirt. "Please."

"Please?" he says. He's genuinely confused.

"Give us a minute," Mitzi says.

"Oh," Kelley says. "Okay." He closes the door, as if this were a reasonable request.

He hears their voices, but they are too faint for Kelley to make out a single word. The doors at the Winter Street Inn are all solid oak; when they were renovating, Kelley insisted on extra insulation in the walls. He never wanted to hear anything going on in any of the rooms. He would, however, like to hear the conversation between George and his wife right now.

At that moment, Isabelle comes bustling down the hall with a stack of fluffy white towels for room 10. They are Turkish cotton, replaced every year, one of the many reasons why Kelley is going broke.

Isabelle stops when she sees Kelley standing outside the door. She has worked at the inn for the past six months, and, although she has proven astute at reading Kelley's moods and attitudes, apparently something about his posture now perplexes her.

"*Qu'est-ce que c'est?*" she asks.

One of the reasons Kelley and Mitzi hired Isabelle was because they both decided they wanted to try to learn French, but half a year later, this is the only phrase Kelley understands. *What is it?* Or, literally, *What is it that it is?*

There is no way to explain it in English, or French, or any other language. Kelley thinks, *I saw Mitzi kissing Santa Claus,* and he starts to laugh in a manic, unhinged way. Isabelle smiles uncertainly.

Kelley says, "George won't be needing those towels."

"Ah?" Isabelle says. "Are you sure?"

"Yes," he says. "I'm sure."

AVA

The dismissal bell rings, and chaos ensues—as bad as the last day of school, if not worse. Today, the kids are hopped up on sugar—hot chocolate, cookies, candy canes—and there is the allure of Santa Claus and presents, presents, presents! Also, there are coats to zip, and hats, scarves, and mittens to keep track of. Ava picks up two stray mittens between the auditorium and the school entrance. She drops them on the table outside the main office. Lost and found, to be dealt with "next year."

Ava is hoarse, and her fingers ache. If she never plays "Jingle Bells" again, it will be too soon. It is, hands down, the least interesting carol ever written. *Why does everyone love it so?* She feels like Sisyphus with his boulder; she will have to play it *at least* one more time, at the annual Christmas Eve party at the inn. There will be no escaping that.

Still, there is something magical about the afternoon. The sky is sterling silver, the air shimmering with mist. It's chilly but probably too warm for snow. Ava stands at the flagpole and waves to her students, who are waving madly back at her through the fogged-up windows of the school bus.

Merry Christmas, Miss Quinn, Merry Christmas, Merry ChristMAS!

How Ava longs to be eight again! Or, no, not eight but five. She was five years old the Christmas before her parents split.

Ava sees Claire Frye, wearing a long red coat and a matching red hat set precariously on top of her dark curls, run into her father's arms. Her father, Gavin Frye, who looks like the pirate Bluebeard, picks Claire up and swings her around so that her hat sails through the air and hits the damp pavement. Gavin retrieves Claire's hat and from his pocket pulls a wax paper bag that Ava knows has come from the Nantucket Bake Shop. Claire discovers two elaborately frosted sugar cookies inside—one Santa, one Rudolph. She chooses Santa and promptly eats his ear. Gavin munches Rudolph's antlers and offers his daughter his arm, like a nineteenth-century gentleman caller.

Ava gets choked up. Claire's mother was hit by a car in September; she died in the ambulance on the way to the hospital. This will be Claire and Gavin's first Christmas without her. If *they* can get into the spirit of the holiday, well then, so can Ava. If she has to play "Jingle Bells" a hundred more times this season, she will do so in Claire Frye's honor.

Ava doesn't check her cell phone until she is sitting in the front seat of her red Jeep Wrangler with the engine running, the heater cranked, and her seat belt fastened. This is her pointless ritual; she wants to be ready for a collision with reality in the event that her phone doesn't tell her what she wants to hear. Which, thanks to her crazy family and her maddeningly aloof boyfriend, it rarely does.

Deep breath. She presses the damn button.

A text from her mother, who tends to treat text messages like handwritten letters, down to the impeccable punctuation: *Hello, sweetheart! I'm in the car, headed to the studio. I miss you. Your paper angel is the only holiday decoration in my apartment. I'm off to Maui tomorrow; I'll be staying at the Four Seasons. I'll send you a ticket if you'd like to escape the winter wonderland...? Daddy sounded like even HE was tempted. (Mitzi must have bought a particularly ugly sweater this year—laughing out loud!) I love you, sweetie! Xoxo, Mom*

Ava closes her eyes and envisions her mother's three-bedroom apartment on the thirty-second floor of a luxury building on Central Park West—sumptuous and soulless.

Ava has no doubt that what her mother says is true; Margaret Quinn is far too busy to deal with Christmas decorations, except for the paper-angel ornament Ava made in second-grade Sunday school at Holy Trinity Episcopal, on East Eighty-Eighth Street, back when her parents were parenting and cared about things like religious education. Back when they lived in the happy, messy brownstone between York and East End. Margaret has saved the angel all these years in an uncharacteristic show of sentimentality. The angel would be dangling by fishing line in one of the floor-to-ceiling windows overlooking the park, or it would be resting inside a six-thousand-dollar Dale Chihuly glass bowl on the ten-thousand-dollar coffee table carved from a single piece of teak harvested from an ancient southeast Asian forest.

Ava loves her mother and yearns for her even now, at age twenty-nine. Ava can see her mother on channel 3 every weeknight at six o'clock, but that's hardly the same thing; in fact, it makes Ava's longing worse, so she avoids watching the nightly news.

A text from Mitzi: *I'm so sorry.*

Sorry for what? Ava wonders. But she deletes the message. She will have too much Mitzi as it is over the holiday break.

A text from her brother Kevin: *Stop by the Bar on your way home.*

Tempting.

A text from her brother Patrick: *Something came up, Jen and kids headed west, I'm staying in the city for Christmas.*

What? Ava reads the text twice, thinking there must be a mistake. She doesn't care if she sees Patrick or not. As the firstborn, he tends to be bossy, bordering on dictatorial, and he's egregiously mercenary—all he seems to care about anymore is money, money, money—but Ava can't believe her nephews aren't coming. What is Christmas without children? She nearly calls Patrick, but she knows he won't answer while the stock exchange is still open.

Item 5: a missed call from her father (no message). Weird, because he knows she is unreachable until three o'clock, and if he needs her to pick up eggs or sugar or food coloring or bananas for the inn, he'd better speak to her in person, or she'll conveniently tell him that she stopped by the Bar to see Kevin and never got the message.

Finally, she scrolls down to the name she has been hoping for. Nathaniel Oscar, labeled in her phone by his initials, NO. There are three text messages from NO, and Ava's heart sinks. Three messages means bad news.

6 a. *Decided to head home after all, taking 1:30 flt, renting car.*

6 b. *Hyannis. Going to Panera for chipotle ckn xtra mayo.*

6 c. *Don't be mad, Mom laid guilt trip. Back next wk, ill call. Xxx*

"Arrraugh!" Ava starts to yell, but her voice is so strained from singing carols that she can barely get the sound out. She watches her favorite group of fifth-grade boys run for the ice rink, with their hockey skates slung over their shoulders. She honks the horn at them, and they see her and wave. *Merry Christmas, Miss Quinn, Merry ChristMAS!* Liam tackles Joel, and Darian steals Jarrett's hat. Not a one of them can carry a tune, and yet they talk incessantly about starting a rock band.

Ava adores them and hopes they grow up to be considerate boyfriends and thoughtful husbands.

Nathaniel is probably halfway to Greenwich by now. There are many things wrong with this scenario. Ava won't be with Nathaniel for Christmas, he clearly won't be proposing, the way she has hoped and prayed for every night (she prays to St. Jude, the patron saint of desperate causes), and he won't provide an escape from the nuthouse that is the Winter Street Inn. He won't be gamely singing along as she plays "Jingle Bells" for the ten zillionth time or handing out cups of Mitzi's horrendous spiced cider (so heavy on the cloves, it's nearly undrinkable). No…instead, he will be in the enormous stone house where he grew up, in Greenwich, Connecticut, with his parents, his two sisters, and their kids. He will be half a mile down the road from Kirsten Cabot, his high school girlfriend, who is recently divorced and home for the holidays.

Ava only knows this last piece of information because she accidentally stumbled across Nathaniel's open Facebook page on his computer while he was in the shower a few days ago.

The message from Kirsten had read: *Please come home,*

I need a shoulder to cry on. Budweiser cans in the backseat of your dad's car like old times?

When Ava saw that, Nathaniel had yet to respond, but Ava knows now what decision he made.

Ava doesn't *want* to love Nathaniel Oscar; she doesn't *want* to want to marry him and give birth to five or ten of his progeny in rapid succession, but she can't seem to help how she feels.

She considers herself a pretty together young woman. Teaching music at Nantucket Elementary School gives her enormous satisfaction. She loves her students and her classroom—the upright piano, tuned the first day of every month, the vintage turntable where she plays her classes the Beatles and Frank Sinatra. In the age of iTunes, Ava has realized, someone has to give the kids a musical education, someone has to teach them the classics. When she held up a vinyl copy of *Revolver,* borrowed from her father's collection, not a single child knew what it was.

"It's a *record,*" Ava said.

And they *still* didn't know!

Ava also loves living at the inn; it's not dissimilar from her dorm in college. She is a social bird and loves it when the inn is filled with guests. There is always someone new to talk to, always someone who wants Ava to play the piano so he or she can sing. Ava even likes living with her family—her brother Kevin, her brother Bart, and Kelley and Mitzi.

Bart is gone now, of course—to Afghanistan—which pains her.

Ava checks her phone again, wondering why there is still no word from Bart. She texted him four days ago. When he left for Germany, he promised he would always respond as soon as he could, and he always has, until Friday, when he deployed. Ava checks her e-mail—nothing. *Well, he's at war now, so he's busy—that's probably not even the right way to describe it—and maybe there's no cell service in Afghanistan?*

Still, she sends another text. It says: *I miss you, Baby Butt. Please let me know you're alive.*

This text bounces back: *Undeliverable.*

Ava wants to scream again. No one in her life is cooperating!

She rereads Nathaniel's texts. *Chipotle ckn xtra mayo* is what the two of them order every time they go to Panera. Ava *introduced* Nathaniel to the chipotle chicken; it's their sandwich, their chain restaurant, their tradition. One of the reasons Ava knows she's in love with Nathaniel is that she loves doing regular, everyday things with him. She loves eating lunch at Panera in the crappy Hyannis strip mall with him; she loves waiting in line at the post office with him. She *loves* curling up in his arms on his brown corduroy sofa and watching holiday movies. *Trading Places* is their favorite. At least a dozen times in the past three weeks he has answered the phone by saying, "Looking good, Billy Ray!"

And she has answered, *"Feeling* good, Louis!"

In addition to being her lover, he is also her friend.

But now, it's two days before Christmas, and he's gone. "Eeeeeeearrgh!" Ava screams.

There's a knock on her window, and she jumps. She wipes away the fog her breath is causing, and there stands Scott Skyler, the assistant principal, in just his shirt and tie— no winter coat. She cranks down her window.

"Hi, Scott," she says.

"You okay?"

"Yes," she says. "Not really. Nathaniel went home."

"Oh boy," Scott says. Scott has served as Ava's confidant for the past twenty months, which isn't really fair, as Scott harbors a crush on Ava that apparently only grows stronger the more she talks about Nathaniel.

"Want to go to the Bar?" she asks. A beer and a shot with Scott and her brother—maybe two shots, since, in addition to the Nathaniel problem, she misses Bart, and her mother, and there will be no adorable nephews to open the gifts she spent hundreds of dollars on—seems like the only thing in the world that will improve her mood.

"I can't," he says. "I'm serving dinner at Our Island Home tonight. Salisbury steak. You're welcome to join me."

Ava lets a single tear drip down her face. Even Scott is busy. He is a tireless do-gooder, something Ava loves about him. She tries to imagine any one of her three brothers serving Salisbury steak at Our Island Home and comes up empty.

"You're coming over tomorrow night, though, right?" she says.

"Wouldn't miss it," Scott says, and he reaches over to catch the tear, a tender gesture that only starts Ava crying harder.

She wipes at her face with her palms and says, "Screw it, I'm going to get drunk."

"Okay," Scott says. "Maybe I'll see you later." He hurries back into the school, and Ava realizes that he only came out to the parking lot to check on her. Sweet, sweet man, great friend, but not her type. By which she means, not Nathaniel. She is sunk. Sunk!

She will go to the Bar.

Then her phone quacks and she thinks, *Nathaniel!*

No such luck. It's her father.

"What?" Ava barks into the phone. She loves her father, but he has the disadvantage of being constantly available and, because she still lives at the inn, *always around,* and hence he has to deal with her darker moods.

Kelley says nothing for a second, and Ava wonders if he's going to reprimand her for being rude, or if he's calling to tell her that Patrick has canceled, or if—God forbid—something has happened to Bart.

"Daddy?" Ava says.

"Mitzi left," Kelley says. "She moved out."

MARGARET

She reads the briefing sheet: four troops killed in Afghanistan, an apparent serial killer in Alaska strangling Inuit girls with piano wire, rumbles heard from Mount St. Helens for the first time in nearly thirty-five years, and SkyMall declares bankruptcy.

"Boring," she says to Darcy, her assistant. "Or am I just jaded?"

"Boring is good," Darcy reminds her. "It's Christmas."

So it is. Margaret looks around the newsroom: There are tabletop trees and strings of colored lights draped over cubicles. There are fake wrapped presents in a studious pile on top of the filing cabinet; those empty boxes sit in a storage closet for eleven months, gathering dust, until Cynthia, the office manager, brings them out the Monday after Thanksgiving. This thought strikes Margaret as unbearably sad. In so many ways, her life is an empty box, prettily wrapped.

But no, she won't go there. She is due in Wardrobe, something green or red tonight, unfortunately. Both colors wash her out.

When was the last time Christmas meant something? she wonders. She has to harken back twenty-four years, to when the boys were in middle school and Ava was five years old, with her freckles and bobbed haircut, wearing her pink flannel nightgown with the lace at the collar. Margaret can picture her clear as day, creeping down the stairs of the brownstone, finding Margaret and Kelley passed out on the sofa in front of the dying embers of the fire after drinking too many Golden Dreams. Thankfully, they had put out the presents and remembered to eat the cookies left for Santa. Ava had unhooked her stocking and come to open it in Margaret's lap, *ooh*ing and *ahh*ing at even the smallest item—the compact, the root beer lip gloss, the lavender socks with polka dots. Margaret inhaled the scent of Ava's hair and petted her soft cheek; nothing had been more delicious than the feel of her children's skin. And then, a while later, the boys would trudge down—plaid pajama pants and Yankees T-shirts, mussed hair, deepening voices, smelly feet, the two of them splay legged on the floor, ripping open their gifts while Kelley paged slowly through the David McCullough biography and Margaret excused herself to pour a glass of really good cold champagne and stick the standing rib roast in the oven. Their Jewish neighbors, the Rosenthals, came for dinner every year, and Kelley's brother, Avery, came up from the Village with his partner, Marcus.

That had been Christmas.

No one in the newsroom would believe that Margaret Quinn had ever cooked a standing rib roast.

This year, when Margaret finishes with the broadcast at seven thirty p.m. on the twenty-fourth, her driver, Raoul, will take her to Newark, where she will fly first-class to Maui, for five luxurious days in a suite at the Four Seasons. Drake is supposed to fly in and meet her, although he has yet to fully commit, which Margaret, perhaps more than any other woman in the world, understands. (An earthquake in California, another school shooting, an assassination attempt, or a dozen things less serious could instantly quash Margaret's vacation plans.) Drake is a pediatric brain surgeon at Sloan Kettering, and the thing Margaret likes best about him is how busy he is. It's a relationship without guilt or expectation; if they both happen to be free, they get together, but if not, no hard feelings. If Drake comes to Maui, they will sleep, have good, fast, goal-oriented sex, and talk about work. Drake likes to drink excellent wine, and he will golf nine holes if Margaret gets off her laptop long enough to go to the spa for her facial and hot-stone massage.

Drake doesn't mind when Margaret is recognized— which she is, everywhere.

It's not exactly Christmas, but it's better than Chinese takeout in her apartment with only Ava's paper angel for company, which is how she's spent some holidays in the recent past.

She's in Wardrobe—green tonight. It's a silk boatneck sheath dress that she thinks makes her look like Vanna White, but Roger, her stylist, says they have to stay in holiday colors. He passed up a silver beaded cocktail dress because he thought it was too Audrey Hepburn.

Margaret yearns for the silver. She says, "Is there really

such a thing as '*too* Audrey Hepburn'?" But Roger won't budge.

She says, "You do know, right, what the Nasty Blogger is going to say about this dress."

"I have never pandered to the Nasty Blogger before," Roger says. "And I'm not doing it tonight. You're wearing the green, my love."

Margaret sighs. There is a blog written by someone called Queenie229, who criticizes Margaret's fashion choices, the color of her hair, and seems to hold a special vendetta against Margaret's watch—a Cartier tank watch with a custom lizard band that Kelley gave her after Ava was born. If Queenie229 can't find anything to particularly dislike about Margaret's outfit, she will resort to picking on what she calls "that hideous watch."

"Please, Roger," Margaret says. "The silver."

Roger ignores her. She takes the green Vanna sheath to the dressing room.

Darcy intercepts her in the corridor. "Message for you," she says. "Kelley."

"Kelley?" Margaret says. "My former husband?"

Darcy nods, and Margaret looks at the pink slip. *Please call immediately.* She thinks of Kelley's son, Bart, who was deployed to Afghanistan last Friday. She thinks of the four soldiers killed that day. *Oh God, no.*

She hands Darcy the green Vanna dress and runs down the hall to her computer, where she brings up the names of the four dead in Afghanistan. None of them Bartholomew Quinn. Hugh exhale of relief. It's something else, then.

She calls Kelley back, even though she really doesn't have time.

He picks up even before the first ring is finished. "Mitzi left me," he says. "She's gone."

KELLEY

It's surprisingly civil, her departure. She steps out of room 10, leaving George behind, and says to Kelley, "I'll go gather my things."

Things? he thinks. He follows her down the hall, past rooms 8 and 9, down the main staircase—the banister wrapped in a garland of fresh greens accented with burgundy velvet bows—then into the main room, where their twelve-foot tree stands. Their tree is decorated with tasteful white lights and whimsical, handmade ornaments—many of them made by "the Christmas Club," a group of women who lived in Mitzi's neighborhood growing up and who fostered Mitzi's love of this holiday—and twenty other ornaments purchased by Kelley especially for Mitzi and given to her each Christmas morning. Is she going to gather those "things"? Is she going to take the ornaments off the tree, leaving it exposed and naked? And what about her nutcracker collection, which has to be one of the most impressive nutcracker collections in all the world, standing guard on the mantel? There is the chef nutcracker, with his toque and whisk, the fireman nutcracker, with his black hat and hose, and this year a United States Marine Corps nutcracker, which Bart thoughtfully purchased for his mother before he left. Is she going to gather those "things"?

What about her crowd of Byers' Choice carolers—the figurines she arranges and rearranges at least twice each season? At the beginning of the month, the carolers were set up on the sideboard as if attending a holiday concert in the village square—the central figures were playing instruments, and the others were gathered to watch and sing along. But now the carolers are set up as if at a bustling market. There is the cheesemonger, a girl selling gingerbread, a rosy-cheeked boy peddling wreaths. Is Mitzi going to gather those "things"? Mitzi loves those carolers; they remind her of being a child and playing with her dollhouse, a grand Victorian her father built her, with seventeen rooms. Kelley has to admit, even he has grown fond of the carolers over the years. When the box comes out of the attic and the figure of "Happy Scrooge" comes out of the box, Kelley feels a sense of delight—it's family tradition that Happy Scrooge is Kelley's favorite, perhaps even a twelve-inch representation of Kelley himself.

Is Mitzi going to walk away with Happy Scrooge?

Mitzi pushes through the French doors into the "back house," where Kelley and Mitzi live with Kevin and Ava and, until this fall, Bart.

From the walk-in linen closet in the hallway, Mitzi pulls out two suitcases.

Kelley says, "Wait a minute, you already packed?"

"Yes," she says.

"You and George have been…planning this?" Kelley says.

"I was hoping to make it through Christmas," she said, "but it didn't work out that way."

"Okay, wait," Kelley said. "Just wait!" His voice is surprisingly stern; it's a tone from his life before, his life on Wall Street and the brownstone on East Eighty-Eighth Street, his life with Margaret and the boys and Ava, back when he was a breadwinner instead of a bread baker, an ass kicker instead of an ass kisser. Quitting his job, leaving Manhattan, marrying Mitzi the Roller Disco Queen of King of Prussia, Pennsylvania, moving to Nantucket year-round, buying a bed-and-breakfast, and having another child—at the age of forty-three—have all made Kelley soft. Wimpy. A pushover. But he isn't about to let his wife run off with 305 pounds of George the Santa Claus until he gets some answers.

"Bedroom," he says. "Now."

"No," she says.

"*Now,*" he says, and she follows him.

Mitzi Quinn, whose real name is also Margaret, is the polar opposite of the original Margaret. *Mitzi is ditzy,* Kelley's kids used to chant, and, Kelley has to admit, she does have her moments. She believes in holistic medicine and chakras and energy work and the healing power of crystals; she reads New Age self-help books, she goes to hot yoga, she never drinks anything stronger than herbal tea, she doesn't eat beef or allow it to be cooked in the house. She is into astrological signs and the lunar calendar, due to the fact that she is a member of the population who was born on Leap Day. Mitzi wears flowing clothes, mostly silk and linen, and cashmere in the winter. Her clothes are unreasonably expensive, and she likes to wear something different every day of the month, another reason Kelley is going broke.

How did she limit herself to two suitcases? he wonders.

He says, "So, what, you're in love with George? George the Santa Claus? You do understand how ridiculous I find this? He's an old man!"

"He's only sixty-six," she says.

Sixty-six? Four years older than Kelley? Is that possible? To Kelley, George seems at least a decade older. Mitzi is only forty-six, so George *is* too old. But Kelley can tell this argument is futile.

"How long has it been going on?" he asks.

She stares him dead in the eye; there is no evasion or fear, only the beautiful blue-gray irises he fell for twenty-one years earlier. Mitzi has eyes like the disco ball that used to spin over the wooden rinks of her youth. Her eyes emit light and color—flashes of green, blue, silver.

"The whole time," Mitzi says.

"What do you mean the *whole time?*" Kelley says. "You mean, twelve years? Since George started staying with us?"

"Yes," Mitzi says.

"You are KIDDING me!" Kelley shouts.

Mitzi doesn't flinch, even though that is most certainly the only time Kelley has ever screamed at her. Kelley and the original Margaret used to have raging arguments with legendary cursing and yelling—once, notably, in the back of a New York City cab, when the driver dumped them out on a sketchy block near St. Mark's Place, saying, *You both crazy!*

Mitzi doesn't care for venting her anger this way; she thinks it's unhealthy and that unkind words can cause permanent psychic damage. This is why Bart was rarely reprimanded and never, ever spanked, which has led him to grow up spoiled, which landed him in heaps of trouble as a teenager, which eventually ended with him joining the Marines (he was low on other reasonable options), and now might very well place him in the line of danger.

"No," Mitzi says calmly. "Not kidding. Twelve years, but only when he was staying here. I mean, it's not like I flew off to meet him in St. Tropez."

"Is that supposed to make me FEEL BETTER?" Kelley shouts.

"Kelley," Mitzi says.

"What?"

"Lower your voice."

"So what now? You're moving *out?* You're going to *Lenox* to live with *George the Santa Claus?*"

"Yes," Mitzi says.

"And that's it?" Kelley says. "We're splitting? Getting divorced?"

"Yes," Mitzi says.

Kelley can't believe this. He can't *believe* it! A thousand thoughts collide: Mitzi, a woman Kelley watched transform from the Roller Disco Queen of King of Prussia, Pennsylvania, into a warm, inviting innkeeper here on Nantucket, beloved by the guests because she cared about their lives, remembered their kids' names, and asked about their hip replacements, is leaving him. Another divorce, another failure; he can't believe it, he didn't even realize there was anything wrong aside from the obvious: the precarious state of their finances, and Bart in Afghanistan. Kelley can't keep from thinking this behavior has to do with Bart; Bart is Mitzi's north star, he is her reason. She has always put Bart's needs and interests and desires before anyone else's. Mitzi has been hysterical since Bart left for Germany in October, even though he was keen to go. Bart has always been a risk taker, which historically landed him in a lot of trouble. Being in the Marine Corps seems to have whipped him into shape. All of his texts and e-mails from Germany exclaimed how much he loved rules; he was thriving under strict discipline and, in fact, craved more (confirming Kelley's theory that one always wants what one doesn't have). Bart's unit, the lowliest of the low, woke up at 0500 hours, and their every move was prescribed until they went to bed, at 2300 hours. Bart was, in his own words, "Slaying every goddamned dragon like St. George." Kelley wasn't quite sure what he was talking about, so he checked Google, which educated him. When Kelley later e-mailed, Bart confirmed that during a weekend of R&R in Munich, he had visited the Alte Pinakothek, where he had seen the Altdorfer painting of St. George slaying the dragon. The Alte Pinakothek had been recommended by Bart's drill sergeant, Sergeant Corbo, because Germany wasn't only beer gardens and bratwurst, it also contained culture, and the soldiers might as well avail themselves of it while they had the chance.

Bart goes to art museums now, Kelley thinks. He runs ten miles in combat boots without complaining, and he does it faster than anyone else in his unit. He scales walls, he can do a one-handed push-up, he's learning how to box, and he knows how to shoot a variety of weapons. He speaks a little German and he wants to learn Arabic. He is using basic geometry, a subject he barely passed his sophomore year. *If I had known it was going to come in handy, I would have paid closer attention!* he wrote.

All of this, Kelley knows, is horrifying to Mitzi. Her baby is shooting guns! And, probably, eating hamburger! Kelley knows that Bart doesn't tell Mitzi half of what he tells Kelley, and that Kelley is to keep certain things on the down low, between them, as father and son, as men.

Such as: Bart will be working with Afghan national security to take down insurgent strongholds and prevent a Taliban takeover when U.S. troops withdraw.

Mitzi's acting out over Bart's deployment makes a certain kind of sense. But she's been boinking George for *twelve years!* While George was *staying with them!* In other words, the love affair was happening under Kelley's own roof, under Kelley's nose! On Christmas Eve! On Christmas Day! It has been going on every Christmas since Bart was seven or eight years old—just like in the movie *Same Time, Next Year,* with Alan Alda and Ellen Burstyn, a movie Kelley actually enjoyed when he saw it a million years ago with the original Margaret.

Margaret told Kelley not to marry Mitzi; she thought Mitzi was silly and too young. *I don't know what you're thinking, Kelley. She's going to want children, and you can't even care for the ones we have now.* Kelley heard Margaret loud and clear, but he surprised her—and himself—by not only marrying Mitzi but by quitting the rat race, leaving Manhattan, taking custody of the children, and moving them to Nantucket. And buying the inn, which was Mitzi's dream.

Although, to be fair, it had been a dream for both of them. It started out, perhaps, as a grandiose gesture of love. Mitzi had stayed at the Winter Street Inn for a dozen years before she met Kelley, and she had watched it fall into decline and decrepitude. When Kelley bought the inn for her, as a wedding present, really, the idea had been that they would embark on a new life together. This inn, built in 1873, originally belonging to the town's grocer, needed *a lot* of work to make it a destination of "high-end comfort"—the sumptuous marble bathrooms, the thick Turkish towels, the four-poster king-size beds made from solid cherry, the pillow-top mattresses, the original paintings by Nantucket artists. Not to mention central air-conditioning, an inn-wide stereo system, plasma TVs and iPod docking stations, and L'Occitane toiletries. Restoring the inn had been expensive and stressful.

So... it hadn't always been the two of them holding hands, skipping along in golden sunshine, but it had been good. They renovated and restored, they advertised and marketed, they married and procreated. Kelley *liked* being an innkeeper. He liked his great stone hearth and his deep leather club chairs and the stairs that creaked because their treads were almost a hundred and fifty years old. He liked packing up box lunches that his guests could take to the beach. He liked tuning up the fleet of eight vintage Schwinns for their guests to ride into town. He enjoyed meeting new people and providing them with a respite from their normal lives. And he loved being a hands-on father to Bart—and, a bit belatedly, to his older kids.

Buying the inn and being with Mitzi and raising his

family on Nantucket Island had brought Kelley real happiness, the kind of happiness he had been so certain he would never find again.

But now, Mitzi is leaving.

Kelley sinks onto their bed. The room smells like Christmas. At night, when they get ready for bed, Mitzi lights her favorite Fraser fir candle. A few weeks ago—the Saturday night of Stroll weekend—Kelley and Mitzi made love by the low flicker of this candle.

He didn't know anything was wrong.

George the Santa Claus.

"Is it *me?*" he asks. "Did I *do* something?"

Mitzi doesn't respond, and Kelley experiences a moment of weakness in which he thinks of asking George and Mitzi to stay through Christmas. The inn needs its Santa Claus, and Kelley needs his business partner. How is he going to throw the party tomorrow night? And what about Christmas dinner?

But no. No. Twelve years. Under his own roof! How could he not have known?

Mitzi gives him a rueful smile. "It's not you, Kelley," she says. "It's me."

"What about the rest of your stuff?" he asks. "What about all your...your *Christmas* stuff?"

She gives him a quizzical look.

"Your ornaments, your nutcrackers...your carolers, for God's sake!"

"Oh," she says. "I'll leave those for the rest of you to enjoy." And with this, she walks out of their bedroom, shutting the door quietly behind her.

PATRICK

Jennifer and the boys get into a taxi headed to Logan Airport, and Patrick watches them from the second-floor picture window, peering around the thirteen-foot Christmas tree, which took Jen and her assistant, Penelope, five hours to decorate with three thousand ornaments and 650 white lights.

Jen did not take the news well. There were forty minutes of screaming into a pillow, forty minutes of muffled sobbing on the phone to her mother (Patrick desperately trying to hear how much she was giving away), and then thirty minutes in a scalding-hot shower before Jen emerged with the news that she was taking the boys to San Francisco for Christmas, even though it's their year to go to Nantucket.

Patrick is mute. He deserves at least this. He tries not to think about the cost of four last-minute plane tickets to the West Coast on the twenty-third of December, or about the bill for the hot water. Such things have never bothered him before because he makes a tremendous amount of money running the private-equity division of Everlast Investments. But now, Patrick has a sick, sick feeling that the well is about to dry up.

He was careful about how he worded things with Jen, although his appearing at the house at eleven o'clock in the morning pretty much said it all. To make matters worse, she thought for an instant that he had taken off from work early so he could go Christmas shopping, or so they could go for a couple's massage before the Everlast Christmas party that evening.

He said, *We're not going to the Christmas party.*

He then explained that he has been placed on a "leave of absence" until after the first of the year, and that his boss, Gary Grimstead, who is a great guy, asked him not to come to the Everlast Investments holiday party.

Because Patrick is under investigation by Everlast's Compliance Department, and Gary thinks it's best for Patrick to lie low until whatever they're looking into blows over.

What are they looking into? Jen asked Patrick.

Patrick asked the same thing of Gary Grimstead, but, although Gary is truly a great guy, he tends to play his cards close to the chest, and he wouldn't exactly say. *Probably the perks,* Gary said. Meaning the "gifts" from clients that Patrick has received in the past eighteen to twenty-four months: private jets to South Beach to golf, floor seats for the Celtics, front-row seats for Billy Joel, trips to Vegas with comped penthouse suites. Those he can feasibly explain away because he is hardly alone in the industry in accepting perks (although the trip to South Beach—a bachelor party for his deputy, Michael Bell—included three Playboy models, and he can't have Jen finding out about that). But then, as he was walking out of Gary's office, smarting from being uninvited to the Four Seasons that evening, he received a text message from an unidentified number that he knew belonged to the temporary cell phone of Bucky Larimer, his fraternity brother from Colgate. Back in September, Bucky had given Patrick key pieces of inside information about a leukemia drug called MDP. Bucky had assured Patrick that the drug was amazing and FDA approval was pending. *A sure thing,* Bucky told Patrick. *It's going to change not only leukemia but maybe cure all cancers, man.* In the past three months, Patrick has invested over twenty-five million dollars of his clients' money in Panagea, the company that makes MDP, and he invested money for Bucky Larimer as well, under the protection of Theta Chi Nominal Trust, named after their fraternity. Patrick is the trustee. It's insider trading, and if Patrick gets caught, he is going to jail.

Patrick tells Jen that Compliance is probably going to slap him on the wrist for taking the perks but that they might find other things they don't like.

Such as...? Jen asked.

He then told her about the leukemia drug, and about how he hedged his bets on it, which is why they call it a hedge fund. Then, because he can't lie to Jen, he tells her that the way he invested the money wasn't exactly legal, because he had privileged pieces of information, provided by someone he knows in the pharmaceutical industry.

He said, *Really, honey, the less you know about the specifics, the better.*

Which was when Jen flipped out. *You might lose your job,* she said. *You might get in real trouble, Patrick. And think about the* public humiliation.

She said this to get a reaction. Patrick is very proud of his good name.

He closed his eyes and shook his head, which Jen understood to be a dismissal of her and her concerns.

As the taxi disappears down Beacon Street, Patrick gazes across the Common. He can see the skaters on Frog Pond and all the twinkling lights in the trees. Diagonally across the Common is the Four Seasons, where Patrick will not be headed this evening. Gary Grimstead is probably picking out his cuff links right this second. In a little while, the Bristol Lounge will hold 150 Everlast employees, who will all be talking about one thing and one thing only.

Patrick Quinn, fingered by Compliance.

Patrick goes to the freezer and pulls out a frosted bottle of Triple 8 vodka; then he walks down the hallway, to the master suite. He has a prescription bottle containing thirteen Vicodin, left over from when he tweaked his back playing tackle football in the front yard of the Theta Chi house at his fifteen-year Colgate reunion, which was where the conversation with Bucky Larimer got going in the first place.

He goes back out into the living room and turns off all the lights except for those on the tree. The tree is beyond beautiful; it's artwork. Jen likes glass balls set all the way back, nearly to the trunk of the tree, and then a second ornament placed midway on the bough, and then the best ornaments—the Christopher Radkos, and Jen's favorites, a fancy fur-clad shopper and a dapper doorman by Soffieria De Carlini—on the ends of the branches, where everyone can appreciate them. In this way, the tree looks full and rich; the glass balls catch the light and the tree seems to glow from within.

Jennifer has serious talent as an interior designer. Their impeccably restored five-story townhouse on Beacon Street, with a roof garden from which they can view the Esplanade and the fireworks every Fourth of July, was just featured on the Beacon Hill Holiday House Tour, and won first place. Jennifer and her assistant, Penelope, garnered three new commissions—one of them a soup-to-nuts job on Mount Vernon Street, and one a renovation of a seven-thousand-square-foot house on Brattle Street in Cambridge, Julia Childs's old neighborhood. Jennifer was swooning with her success, and Patrick, trying to be supportive of her burgeoning career, popped a bottle of Billecart-Salmon, then called the sitter and took her to dinner at Clio.

That, a mere ten days ago.

Today, the third-shortest day of the year, it is fully dark at four o'clock.

One shot of vodka, two Vikes. Patrick is still in his suit, but he takes his shoes off and reclines on the sofa.

He has left himself exposed. He is such an IDIOT!

He can't stand to think about it, but he can't think about anything else. If the stuff about MDP comes to light, he will be written about in the *Globe* and possibly the *Wall Street Journal*. Jennifer will lose her clients, and the boys will have to go to public school. Patrick will never get hired anywhere else in Boston. He isn't the kind of person who has a "second act" in him; he is the kind of person who sets a path and then follows it. Except he deviated from the path, and now he will pay. They will have to sell the house and move... where? To Kansas City, where Patrick will manage the branch of a local bank? Would a local bank in Kansas even be able to hire him? The inside information and the subsequent investing might qualify as a felony. Possibly. He should get a lawyer, but that's an admission of defeat, right?

Patrick doesn't know who he's kidding. Public humiliation isn't the worst thing. Going to jail is the worst thing.

His mother's name will be dragged through the mud. He hasn't considered this until now. Oh God. Margaret Quinn's son: cheat, liar, crooked good-for-nothing scoundrel. Playboy models, insider trading, placing bets on a drug for sick children.

Another shot of vodka.

His phone lights up with a text message, and then immediately a second and third text message. *It's Jen,* he thinks. She got to Logan but couldn't bring herself to board the plane. They've been together fourteen years and have never spent a Christmas apart. If she comes back, he might survive.

But the text messages aren't from Jen. There's one from his father, one from his sister, and one from his brother Kevin.

Dad: *Mitzi left.*

Ava: *At Bar with Kev. Mitzi left Daddy. We need you to come home.*

Kevin: *Dude, come home.*

Patrick reads the three messages again, but his head is swimming with the vodka and the Vicodin. Mitzi *left?* For where? He gets confused, thinking of Jen at Logan, sipping a glass of good chardonnay at Legal Test Kitchen while the kids play on their iDevices at the gate. Patrick closes his eyes and pictures the Bar, where his brother Kevin works. Kevin is the happiest person in the family, and Ava, a music teacher at the elementary school, is second. They never felt any pressure to earn or achieve or propagate the Quinn family name—because they always had Patrick to do it for them. They don't even particularly *like* Patrick, he doesn't think. He's only ninety minutes away, but they never come to Boston to visit; they think Patrick is a carbon copy of the relentless bastard their father used to be before he quit his big, important job in New York and bought the inn on Nantucket and became a nice guy. Probably, when Ava goes to the Bar to have a beer with Kevin, all they do is talk about what a tool Patrick is. They need him now because there's a crisis—*Mitzi left*—and neither of them is a problem solver. Patrick is the problem solver, always.

But what they don't know is that Patrick can't help today.

His phone accidentally drops to the floor with a clatter, but Patrick can't summon the energy to retrieve it. Even though he knows they don't like him as much as they like each other or Bart, there is still something appealing to Patrick about walking into the Bar to have a beer with his siblings. But he's in no condition, and they don't want him anyway, not really. If Bart were on Nantucket, Patrick would go, but Bart is in Afghanistan, nobly serving their country. Bart grew up idolizing Patrick—beyond Big Papi, beyond Santa Claus, beyond God. What would Bart think of him now? He would realize that Patrick is a little man behind a big facade, like the Wizard of Oz. Patrick does another shot of vodka and takes another Vike. Oblivion—how much poison must he ingest to achieve it?

He watches the tree sparkle. Three thousand ornaments. Despite everything, he thinks, it is still so pretty.

AVA

She drinks another beer at the Bar with Kevin, who has to work until closing. He will be no help except in numbing Ava's senses, impairing her judgment, and getting her drunk— but this has always been the case with Kevin. He calls himself the Underachieving Quinn, the slacker, the loser, the Big Zero, names Ava scoffs at, although she realizes that Kevin's sense of worth has suffered from his life choices, many of which have been dictated by his dead-end relationship with Norah Vale, whom Ava always thinks of as Norah Vale the Cautionary Tale.

Kevin and Norah started dating in tenth grade, and they famously became engaged in eleventh grade. Kevin bought Norah a silver claddagh ring, and together, they announced they were going to get married as soon as they turned eighteen.

Kelley, Mitzi, and Margaret had all tried to talk Kevin out of it. Kevin had already been accepted to the University of Michigan; Norah wasn't going to college. She didn't have the grades, or the money, or the interest. None of the parents came right out and said it, but Ava now understands that they didn't think Norah Vale was a quality choice for a life partner. Norah had five older brothers, but only the eldest of the brothers and Norah shared a father; the four boys in between had been sired by two different men. Norah's eldest brother, Danko Vale, was a tattoo artist. He had tattooed a fearsomely realistic python around Norah's neck and shoulders. The head of the snake had been done in trompe l'oeil style, so that it looked like the python was striking from just below Norah's clavicle.

This tattoo had given Ava nightmares. She had never been able to hug Norah Vale, not even on her wedding day.

Norah had gone to Ann Arbor with Kevin, but she was *miserable* there. And so Kevin dropped out after his freshman year, much to the family's consternation. He then enrolled at the Culinary Institute of America in Poughkeepsie. He and Norah lasted three years, although Norah spent much of the third year at home, on Nantucket, working at the Bar. And then, with only a six-month externship to complete, Kevin dropped out of the CIA. He came back to Nantucket and got a job at the Bar, which was like climbing back into his smelly, unmade childhood bed. He had no degree and nothing to show for his years since high school graduation — except his devotion to Norah Vale.

Now, Norah Vale lives in Miami, where Ava is pretty sure she works as a stripper, and Kevin is the manager of the Bar and is hoping to buy it someday from the elderly man who owns it.

Ava loves Kevin. She loves all her brothers and takes a distinct pride in being the hub of their wheel.

"Have you heard from Bart?" Ava asks Kevin.

"Have not."

"No," Ava says. "Me either. What do you think it's like over there?"

"I have no idea," Kevin says.

"Me either," Ava says. "I don't even know if it's hot or cold. I was thinking desert, hot, but Afghanistan is mountainous, too, so maybe it's cold."

"He's in the Marines," Kevin says. "I'm sure he's prepared for both extremes."

"Do you worry about him?" Ava asks.

Kevin smiles at her. "He'll be fine."

He'll be fine. Well, he *has* to be fine, because anything else is unthinkable.

"Have you gotten a response from Patrick?" Ava asks.

"No," Kev says. "You?"

"Of course not," Ava says. Her fifth ice-cold Corona with double limes sits in front of her; she should probably start thinking about getting home for dinner. However, Ava is savoring a secret triumph: Nathaniel has called twice from the road, and she let both calls go to voice mail. She is determined to be present and enjoy being at the Bar with Kevin, especially since it looks like they both might be getting a bona fide family crisis for Christmas. Mitzi has left their father, Patrick isn't coming home, and Bart...Ava can't even think about Bart anymore. Or rather, what she thinks is that if Bart will just text and say he's all right, she'll be able to handle the rest of it.

She says, "What do you think happened with Patrick? Do you think he and Jen split?"

What are the chances, she wonders, of two marriages in the same family falling apart *on the same day?*

"Fight, maybe," Kevin says. "Holiday stress, or her mother is sick, or he was short a couple diamonds in the tennis bracelet. But they didn't 'break up.' They're made for each other."

Ava agrees: Patrick and Jen are one of those couples who are oddly synced in their Type-A-ness. Jennifer is so tightly wound, it makes Ava's head hurt just to look at her, yet Patrick worships her in all her glorious anality.

"Is 'anality' a word?" Ava asks. Kevin has loaded the jukebox with all her favorite holiday songs. Right now, the Boss is singing "Santa Claus Is Coming to Town."

"If it's not, it should be," Kevin says. "With a photo of Jen right next to it. I know that's what you were thinking."

Kevin is the greatest guy on earth, Ava decides. They used to fight when they were younger, which Ava always understood to be a scramble for second place. Patrick always claimed first place.

"How can you tell if two people are made for each other?" Ava asks. She has moved on from anality to deep philosophy. Kevin survived Norah Vale, and this gives him a certain authority when it comes to love and relationships. "What's the criteria, in your opinion?"

Kevin leans his elbows on the bar, dirty rag slung over his shoulder. His hair is a brighter shade of red than she

remembers from when she saw him this morning; his freckles are more pronounced. A string of colored lights twinkles
overhead. The Kinks sing "Father Christmas."

He says, "Not sure. But Patrick and Jen meet the criteria,
whatever it is."

"What about me and Nathaniel?" Ava asks, then hates
herself.

"Nathaniel's a good guy," Kevin says. He heads to the
end of the bar to get another round for the two construction
workers who are the only other people in the place. *Why
aren't there more people here?* Ava wonders. *Because everyone
else is Christmas shopping, or they are, like Nathaniel, headed
south on I-95 in order to celebrate the holidays in the homes
they grew up in, and drink beer in the backseats of cars with
the girls they lost their virginities to.*

Ava feels a scream coming on.

She misses her mother.

She should go to Hawaii with Margaret, she thinks.
Four Seasons Maui. Last year, her mother spent all day in a
chaise longue by the pool, next to Bob Seger. He knew who
Margaret was, but she thought he was just some old hippie
dude from Detroit until the end of their conversation, when
he introduced himself and Margaret asked him to sign a
cocktail napkin for Ava.

Nathaniel is a good guy, but Kevin's answer seems to
indicate that he does not necessarily think Nathaniel and
Ava are made for each other.

Before Ava can ask him or herself why not, someone pulls up a bar stool next to her and says, "Hey, Ava."

Ava turns. It's Scott Skyler.

"Hey," she says. "I thought you were serving dinner at Our Island Home."

"I finished," Scott says. "I was driving home and saw your Jeep, so I thought I'd come in and have one with you."

"You *finished?*" Ava says. "What time is it?"

"Quarter to eight," Scott says.

"Whoa!" Ava says, and she jumps backward off her stool. Where did the afternoon go? She sways on her feet. The Barenaked Ladies are singing "God Rest Ye Merry, Gentlemen." Kevin leaves the construction workers, then drops a Bud Light in front of Scott, and they execute some kind of complicated handshake.

"Ava?" he says. "Another?"

"It's almost eight o'clock!" she says. "I have to get home!"

"You're not driving," Kevin says. "Sorry, sis."

She's about to protest, but she knows he's right.

Scott stands up. "I'll drive you home."

"No," she says. "You stay and enjoy your drink. I'll... walk."

"Walk home?" Kevin says. "No, no, and no."

"I'll take you," Scott says. "I didn't want a beer, anyway. I just wanted to see you."

Ava puts on her coat and dutifully follows Scott out to the parking lot. She can feel her phone vibrating in her purse, but she doesn't check it. She hopes it's Nathaniel, she hopes he understands she's hurt that he left the island without saying good-bye or Merry Christmas. He prides himself on his freedom and spontaneity, his ability to fly by the seat of his pants. But Ava wishes he felt more of a sense of commitment to her. She wishes that, since it's *Christmas,* he'd had a bit more foresight. Just twenty-four hours earlier, he cooked her dinner at his cottage, as he did every Monday night in football season, so they could watch the game together. He made white chili and corn muffins, and tapioca pudding, because it's Ava's favorite dessert from childhood. The evening had been wonderful, just like every evening with Nathaniel. But if Ava had known he was leaving today, she would have suggested they exchange presents, or do something else to mark the holiday together.

Did Nathaniel not think of these things because he was male, and therefore oblivious? Or did she just not matter to him? He had made her tapioca pudding, and then, at half-time, he threw her over his shoulder and carried her into his bedroom, where he devoured her like a starving man. So he did love her. But then today, he just *left*—either because his mother's entreaties got to him, or because Kirsten Cabot sent another message on Facebook too enticing to resist.

Ava emits a long, loud, confused sigh, which Scott ignores. He takes her arm and gently helps her up into the passenger seat of his Explorer.

She shivers in her seat until Scott starts the engine and

cranks the heater. *I just wanted to see you.* There isn't any ambiguity where Scott Skyler's feelings are concerned. He likes her, he has always liked her, but he has accepted the role of best friend, and for that, Ava is grateful.

"I hate 'Jingle Bells,' " she says. "I've always hated it."

"Yeah," Scott says. "Me too."

DECEMBER 24

KEVIN

It's twenty after one in the morning when Isabelle pulls up behind the Bar in her little Ford pickup, a vehicle that has come to define her. Kevin sees the maroon Ranger through the back window, and his blood quickens.

Isabelle has never swung by the Bar to see him before; she's always been convinced it's *"trop dangereux,"* that someone might *"découvrir"* — find out they're seeing each other. Since their relationship began six months ago, Isabelle has been dead set on absolute secrecy, as though they're involved in international espionage. She's convinced that if Kelley and Mitzi find out, they'll fire her. They hired her to teach them French (which she's failed miserably at, but only because Kelley and Mitzi are too busy to learn) and to run the daily operations of the inn (which means cleaning the rooms, doing laundry, and cooking), but if she loses her job, it's back to France — specifically, Montpellier, where her father is unemployed and her mother is depressed.

Montpellier isn't Paris and it's not the Riviera, it's not cafés and cobblestone streets and fat chefs and friendly dogs. It's a city, she says, like New Haven, but without Yale. Like Hartford, but without insurance. (The only place in the U.S. that Isabelle has visited other than Nantucket is Connecticut.) She came to the States to work as an au pair for a family named the Salingers, in Glastonbury, and they brought her to Nantucket for the summer. She loved the island so much that when her time with the Salingers was over, she returned, even though her visa had expired. She originally got a job cleaning houses for a Brazilian woman, but then she met Mitzi at yoga class, and Mitzi—who had a soft spot for orphans and strays—invited Isabelle home and gave her a better job and a room at the inn.

Isabelle and Kevin are madly in love—madly! For Kevin, it's difficult to keep the secret; he doesn't see the point. He has explained to Isabelle a hundred times that his parents will be happy for them, and especially for him, Kevin, who has had such lousy luck with love.

It's a good sign that Isabelle feels safe enough to show up at the Bar tonight. Of course, in the past twenty-four hours, everything has changed.

Kevin locks up the Bar and strolls out to Isabelle's driver's side window, his parka zipped to his chin, his Patriots sideline hat pulled down, his hands stuffed into his jeans pockets. He wants a cigarette. Normally, they would share one.

She looks pale and sick. He can't *believe* how happy he is.

"So...," she says, "*ton père* is a...mess."

"Is he?" Kevin says.

"You do not sound like you *care*," Isabelle says.

"I guess it hasn't sunk in," Kevin says. "Mitzi left."

"Left with George," Isabelle says. "Packed two valises, *c'est tout*. I wonder about *ses couteaux*...her...knives? She treated those knives *comme des enfants,* but I think she's leaving them?"

"She's upset about Bart," Kevin says.

"Well, yes," Isabelle says. "*Évidemment.* Her only child *est à la guerre.*"

Kevin experiences a rush of envy, along with annoyance. Bart joined the Marines after a string of spectacular screwups, and now he's an instant hero. The way Isabelle talks about Bart with such reverence really irritates Kevin. She didn't know him before. Bart is the same kid who stole three cases of beer and half a dozen bottles of Jim Beam out of the Bar while Kevin was working and then proceeded to get drunk with his moronic friends and do donuts on the airport runway until he crashed into the fence, breaking Lance Steppen's femur and totaling the two-year-old LR3 he had borrowed from Kelley and Mitzi without asking.

"I don't think it's that dangerous over there anymore," Kevin says.

"Four soldiers today," Isabelle says. *"Morts."*

"Dead?" Kevin says. *"Really?"* He doesn't follow the news except for ESPN SportsCenter, but he knows Isabelle watches his mother every night at six o'clock, along with the rest of the country. Four soldiers killed—but that will never be Bart. Dad and Mitzi can worry all they want, but Bart has always led a charmed existence, and Kevin knows it will stay this way. Bart's Humvee might roll over a land mine planted by rebel forces outside Sangin, but Bart will do a double somersault and land on his feet, unharmed.

"Yes," Isabelle says. "Anyway, your father is walking in the house like a ghost, not talking, just floating and staring, picking up the sugar bowl, then setting it down. Opening the cabinet that holds *les plats de Noël,* then closing it. Mitzi did not prepare for the soiree tomorrow night. She must have been planning this and assuming Kelley would cancel. So I have been all day preparing hors d'oeuvres. I am going to order cookies from the bake shop. Your father says in secret that Mitzi's cookies are…"

"Inedible," Kevin says. He has a flashback to being a teenager, he and Patrick dropping Mitzi's gingerbread men from their third-story bedroom window. They never broke, never even cracked. "So, is the party still on, then?" Kevin has a hard time imagining the Christmas Eve party happening without Mitzi. She's always the mistress of ceremonies, in her short Mrs. Claus dress—red velour with white fur trim—and her high black-suede boots. Mrs. Claus to George's Santa Claus—Kevin gets it now. He can't believe his father has been so completely cuckolded.

"Oui," Isabelle says. She frowns at him, and then she dissolves into tears.

He wipes her chin with his thumb. "Don't cry," he says. "Please don't cry. It's happy. It's good."

"I do not know what to do!" Isabelle says.

"Hey," he says. "I'm going to help you."

"I do not know what help you are thinking of," Isabelle says. "I might be sent home, Kevin. With our baby."

Just the word, "baby," lights Kevin up. A baby, his baby, his and Isabelle's baby.

She cries into her open palms. Kevin understands what he has to do. He has to ask her to marry him. He should get down on one knee right here in the parking lot. It would change everything. Her tears would dry up immediately.

But...

Many thoughts collide in his mind.

Propose! Ask Isabelle Beaulieu to be his wife! She is *so beautiful,* with her long blond hair, and she is so sweet and kind, hardworking and humble. In six months, his ardor for her has doubled and quadrupled. When he is at the Bar and she is at the inn, he thinks about her nonstop.

But...

He's scared. Scared and scarred. There might as well be stitches in a jagged ring around his heart.

He has heard enough platitudes and received enough "words of wisdom" in regard to Norah Vale to last several lifetimes. *It wasn't meant to be; It's for the best; They're all bitches; Love stinks.* Nothing makes his anguish over what happened with Norah any better. She broke his heart, trashed his dreams, and left him flat broke. She walked away with nine years of his life, ruined his chances for a college degree—twice—and demolished his faith in humankind.

No more women, he vowed.

Then along came Isabelle. The second he saw her smile, the instant he heard her lightly accented voice, he was a goner.

News of the baby, delivered first thing that morning, in a note slipped under his bedroom door, made him whoop like a rodeo cowboy.

"My family will be happy," he says. "We'll just tell everyone the truth: we fell in love, and now we're pregnant."

She cries harder, and Kevin climbs into the passenger side and pulls her into his lap.

A baby, he thinks.

He strokes her hair, and his heart soars. "We'll keep living at the inn," he says. "Just until we get on our feet. Maybe Dad will let us take the family suite on the third floor."

"But what if I get sent back?" Isabelle says. "It is always a danger! And now that I am..."

"It's okay," Kevin says. "That's not going to happen. I'll make sure of it."

"How?" Isabelle says.

He wants to say It. He nearly says it.

But.

MARGARET

Christmas Eve morning, she receives a text from Drake: *All in.*

A wave of relief, followed by excitement. Margaret had been steeling herself for a cancellation from him; she always likes to keep her expectations low to avoid disappointment — but Hawaii will be far superior with Drake along.

Buoyed by this good news, she packs four bikinis, two cover-ups, five sundresses, her straw hat, a copy of Donna Tartt's *The Goldfinch,* which she's been meaning to read for months — and then, because it *is* Christmas, she carefully packs the paper angel that Ava made in second-grade Sunday school, back when Christmas was Christmas, back when Margaret was a mother instead of a national icon.

She calls Kelley and gets his voice mail. Then she calls Ava and gets her voice mail. The only people in America who don't take Margaret Quinn's calls are her own family. She thinks about calling the inn, but for some reason this intimidates her — probably because every other time she's called that number, Mitzi has answered, and, as is to be expected, Mitzi does not appreciate hearing Margaret Quinn's famous voice on the other end of the line. Now, though, Mitzi is gone (can this be true, really?), but even so, Margaret won't call the inn. It's Christmas Eve, and Kelley must be running at capacity, plus throwing that enormous party. If anyone needs Margaret, she supposes they will call.

After she packs, she brews an espresso and sits down at her computer. There are twelve more soldiers dead in Afghanistan. There is some kind of backlash or new order taking action; the U.S. has lost more soldiers in one week than we have since 2004. Margaret's heart clenches as she scans the list. Not Bart.

How do Kelley and Mitzi live like this?

She calls Kelley again, and again gets his voice mail.

PATRICK

In the morning, he is awakened by a pounding on the front door. His head feels like a crumbling plaster cast of a head. It is both heavy and empty, filled with rocks and something that sloshes like liquid. The bottle of vodka has rolled under the coffee table; the pills are lined up on the glass surface. Ten pills left, which means he took only three. His stomach squelches; whoever is at the door is insistent.

It's federal marshals, he thinks. He won't answer, he won't confess, he won't surrender. He won't leave the house; they'll have to storm him like a SWAT team if they want to get him. He is grateful now that Jen decided to leave with the kids; she wouldn't take this well at all—a stranger on the front step, pounding on their door, attracting the attention of the neighbors.

And yet, he misses Jen. He needs her. If she were here, she would go to the door and tell whoever it is to GO AWAY. She can be formidable; Patrick can't imagine anyone intimidating her. Also, Patrick misses the kids—the shooting and helicopter noises of their video games, their screaming and yelling and fighting, their sweet, funky boy smell of sweat and grass and pancake syrup.

Still, the knocking.

Patrick thinks about standing up the way some people think about climbing Mount Everest. Can it be done? He moves his legs to the floor; that much goes okay. The more difficult task is raising his head and torso. *Ohhhhhkay.* He gets to his feet and hobbles over to the picture window.

At the front door is a man in uniform. Patrick hides behind the Christmas tree and thinks: *I'm going to jail.*

The man keeps knocking. He has no intention of going away; Patrick can't escape his fate. Patrick descends the stairs and says, "Who is it?"

"Blahblahblah office," the man says.

Patrick cracks the door, aware that he is still wearing his suit from the day before—minus his tie, his jacket, and his shoes.

"Can I help you?" he asks.

"Patrick Quinn?"

Patrick nods. The man is about fifty-five, plump, and silver haired. Patrick can take him in a fight, he thinks.

The man starts handing Patrick boxes. Patrick is confused. The man is wearing a uniform, vaguely militaristic, but the packages he's giving Patrick seem like regular packages. Patrick tries to focus on the labels—he really needs his glasses, he's so dreadfully hungover—but he makes out *CBS Studios,* and the relief he feels nearly causes him to levitate.

United States Postal Service. These are Christmas gifts, sent to the kids from Margaret. Every year Margaret has her assistant, Darcy, order gifts using some incredible service that always selects the perfect gift for each boy.

"And this," the postal worker says, "requires a signature." He hands Patrick a small cube of a box with luxurious weight. It's caviar from Petrossian, his mother's gift each year to him and Jen. Normally, they eat it on New Year's Eve.

Patrick scribbles his name on the clipboard. He wants to kiss the mailman.

"Thank you!" he shouts. His voice is so loud that the mailman's head snaps back. His voice is so loud, it echoes across the Common.

The mailman retreats down the steps, and Patrick moves all the packages inside and carries the box with the caviar up to the kitchen. He hopes they have eggs. He is going to scramble them all and dump the caviar on top. It will be his breakfast, and Jen's punishment for leaving.

His cell phone rings, but Patrick ignores it. *That* will be Jen, he is certain. But she's the one who left with his kids two days before Christmas, so let her wonder.

Then the house phone rings. Definitely Jen. Patrick finds eight eggs in the fridge and cracks them all in a stainless steel bowl, trying not to dwell on how the sound of the eggs cracking mimics the pain in his head. He adds cream, and salt and pepper; he butters a frying pan. How many times this year has he actually *cooked* in this kitchen? He can't remember any. Jen does the cooking, and she does it perfectly. Everything she makes is fresh and seasonal. She practically reads his mind. On nights he wants roast chicken with her buttery mashed potatoes, there's roast chicken. On nights he wants Cobb salad with grilled lobster, there it is. They have cheese fondue on Valentine's Day, beef and broccoli stir-fry for the Chinese New Year. He misses Jen! He wonders if something bad will happen if he eats the caviar on the wrong day. Well, something bad has *already* happened, which is why he's doing this.

The eggs sizzle. Patrick grabs a wooden spoon. The eggs have to be soft and creamy; otherwise they will not be suitable for this quality of caviar.

Ava and Kevin think he and Jen are food snobs. Kevin's favorite food is the ACK Mack pizza from Sophie T's—located across the street from the Bar—and if it's a day old, so much the better.

The house phone rings again. Jen is desperate. Patrick

likes that at first—he likes the idea of his wife regretting her decision to leave and calling to beg his forgiveness. He moves the eggs around in the pan like an artist dabbing paint on a canvas. He will tell Jen he is about to eat the caviar.

"Hello?" he says.

"Patrick?" a voice says. It's Gary Grimstead. "Man, I need you to sit down."

KELLEY

After the news that Mitzi is leaving him and that he will be getting divorced *again* sinks in, Kelley does the only thing he can do: he drives to Hatch's and buys a bottle of Wild Turkey and a pack of Camels. Then, once back at the inn, he grabs a couple of Cokes from the complimentary guest fridge and heads to his bedroom, where he locks himself in.

It's noon on Christmas Eve. He pours himself a drink and smokes his first cigarette in over two decades. It makes him cough. According to Mitzi, alcohol and tobacco are poison, and he is sure to be on death's door any second.

But right now, it feels good. Or not good, exactly, but rebellious and exciting, which is the most he can hope for.

Inspection of the bedroom leads Kelley to understand that Mitzi has been planning this exodus for a while. She packed only two suitcases to take with her, but every single one of her belongings is gone with the exception of two things. The first is her Mrs. Claus dress, which is probably two or three inches too short for a woman Mitzi's age but which she insisted on wearing to their party every year anyway. Kelley is confused. She ran off with Santa Claus but neglected to pack her matching outfit? Then he remembers her words: *I was hoping to make it through Christmas, but it didn't work out that way.*

So she left the Mrs.-Claus-as-street-worker dress here, just in case.

The other item hanging in the closet is a gold lamé jumpsuit, which Mitzi used to wear to the roller disco and which Kelley hilariously squeezed himself into one long-ago Halloween. Mitzi must have shipped all her other clothes to Lenox. Kelley had noticed her packing up large boxes, but he'd assumed they were Christmas gifts for Bart.

Bart. Kelley has alerted Kevin, Patrick, Ava, and even Margaret about Mitzi's departure, but he has no way to reach Bart other than e-mailing him, which seems cruel. A phone call is in order, surely? He is, after all, the one who will be most affected. Kelley lights another cigarette; he is smoking defiantly, without even a window cracked open. The room will stink for all eternity; as an innkeeper, Kelley knows this.

Kelley wonders for a second if, perhaps, Mitzi has already

broken the news to Bart. Mother and son do share an unusual and possibly unhealthy intimacy, or so Kelley always thought. She was never a mother the way Margaret was a mother, back when Margaret was a mother and not the most famous newsperson in America. Margaret stuck firmly to rules and boundaries—no kids slept in their bed, ever; there were no sleepovers without communication between Margaret and the other parents; there was no grade below a B; and there was a list of rotating chores, the schedule for which was taped to the refrigerator and adhered to. Margaret loved the kids, but she didn't pander to them. Mitzi is another story. She never reprimanded Bart growing up; if he misbehaved, there was always a long, philosophical inquiry as to *why* Bart bit another child / went into the ocean without telling Mitzi / got drunk at the age of fourteen and threw up inside Ava's piano. Mitzi used to walk around naked in front of Bart; she used to tell him when she was menstruating. Kelley wouldn't be surprised if Mitzi had confided her affair to Bart—even years earlier.

Kelley is so incensed by this thought that he pours himself another Wild Turkey and logs on to his computer.

Mitzi has always been the one to keep up the Winter Street Inn Facebook page, but now Kelley takes matters into his own hands. He posts (to all 1,114 of their page's "friends"): *In light of my recent discovery that my wife, Mitzi, has been conducting an affair with George (Santa Claus) for the past twelve years, tonight's party at the Winter Street Inn is canceled.*

And will be canceled for the foreseeable future, he thinks. He's going to sell the inn. God, what a relief it will be— financially and emotionally. He will list it for four million but accept three-five. He will call Eddie Pancik on the twenty-sixth; everyone on island calls him Fast Eddie, which Kelley *hopes* means Eddie Pancik will sell the inn quickly.

But why wait for Eddie Pancik? Kelley wonders as he finishes his drink. He goes back onto the Winter Street Inn Facebook page. His post of a few minutes earlier hasn't gar- nered any "likes," only one comment from Mrs. Gabler, who was Bart's kindergarten teacher and who is the first person to arrive at the Christmas party every year.

Mrs. Gabler's comment says: *Is this some kind of crank call?*

Crank call? Mrs. Gabler is elderly and confused. At the party, she drinks only cognac, and Kelley always keeps a bottle of Rémy Martin on hand just for her. Extravagances abound!

Kelley feels embarrassed that no one else has liked his post, but, of course, who *would* like it? There should be an option to dislike a post. Why hasn't anyone thought of this?

On their Facebook page, Kelley sees, are happy photos of Christmas Eves past, and now that Kelley looks closer, he sees that nearly all the photos on the page include George in his Santa suit, and most of them have Mitzi in the slutty Mrs. Claus dress and her high black-suede boots. There are several photos of George and Mitzi together. This is disgust- ing! How did Kelley not notice this before?

He posts again: *Winter Street Inn FSBO. $4M. Please call...*

He feels better than he has in eons! He pours himself another drink and considers another cigarette but demurs. What else can he do?

He slips the gold lamé jumpsuit off the hanger. He is going to light it on fire. Not in the bedroom—with his luck, the whole house will go up in flames—but in the bathroom. In the bathtub, where the fire will be contained. The claw-foot porcelain tub with antique fixtures that Mitzi insisted on during the renovation, and which cost him four thousand dollars.

For a while, he had believed it was the best four thousand dollars he'd ever spent. He can remember dozens of times when Mitzi would lie in the tub for one of her scented baths—jasmine in the summer, sandalwood in the winter. She would pile her honey-colored curls on top of her head in a bun, and she would read poetry. Poetry was made for the bath, Mitzi believed. She was partial to Pablo Neruda. Kelley can practically hear her reciting to him from "If You Forget Me":

"Ah my love, ah my own, in me all that fire is repeated... my love feeds on your love, beloved."

The air was filled with sweet steam; Mitzi's skin was rosy and glowing from the heat of the water. Kelley often brought her a mug of lemon-ginger tea, and more often than not, she would emerge from the bath and let Kelley help her on with her thick, white robe. She had looked like the subject of a Degas painting but far more lovely.

My love feeds on your love, beloved.

Those days are OVER.

What else can Kelley throw on the fire? Because it's Christmas, he can't bring himself to torch the Mrs. Claus dress, even though the sight of it sickens him. Just as he can't seem to get out the trash can and dump all of Mitzi's carolers and nutcrackers. *I'll leave those for the rest of you to enjoy.* More like, *I'll leave those here to torture you and make you cry.*

Kelley ransacks Mitzi's drawers. She has taken everything. She has, he realizes, taken every family photo that has Bart in it. The only photos left in the bedroom are ones of him and the three olders.

On the top shelf of the closet, he finds the accessories that go with the gold lamé jumpsuit — namely, a gold braided headband and gold wristbands, excellent in their absurdity. He throws them into the bathtub, then wishes for lighter fluid. He finds half an inch of Mitzi's organic hair spray. Will this work? He pours the hair spray over the gold lamé mess, then hits the leg of the jumpsuit with the Kiss lighter he bought at the liquor store. The Kiss lighter resonates with Kelley's sense of irony, and it's even better now that he's using the lighter to set the gold lamé jumpsuit on fire and, along with it, the vision of Mitzi dancing and skating to "Rock and Roll All Nite." The material smolders at first and emits a toxic smell, like something coming out of Jersey City during a sanitation strike in the dog days of summer. Then the fire catches—the organic hair spray is clearly flammable. The jumpsuit curls and crinkles like aluminum foil; the bathroom fills with smoke, and Kelley hurries to open a window, but he has trouble because he installed the storm windows right before Thanksgiving, and they're sticking tight. He turns on the bathroom fan. If the smoke alarms go, the inn will have to be evacuated, and the fire department will come, and Kelley will have some explaining to do.

There is a knock on his bedroom door, which he ignores.

He watches Mitzi's roller disco outfit transform into something even more hideous than it was, if that were possible.

"Daddy!" Ava says. "Open up!"

Ava, his sweetheart, his only little girl. He loves her like crazy, but she has always belonged first to Margaret. In fact, her voice right now sounds just like Margaret's.

"Daddy!" The edge of hysteria, or just extreme impatience. The same tone Margaret used to take when she had to stay late at the studio and she *really needed* Kelley to leave work to go pick up Ava from piano lessons or attend one of the boys' basketball games. *One of us has to be there, and it can't be me!* Well, it couldn't be him either a lot of the time; a lot of the time, the Quinn children had neither parent representing, which was humiliating to everyone involved and ended with Kelley and Margaret fighting, each of them

screaming, *My job is important!* Whose job was *more* important? They could debate that, at 110 decibels, for hours.
Margaret was more visible; Kelley made more money. He
asked Margaret to quit; he wanted her to stay home and
parent. *Why me?* she said. *Because you're the mother,* Kelley
replied. Kelley had been doing a lot of cocaine at that time,
to stay sharp, to stay awake, to constantly monitor the overseas stock markets. It was the late eighties, the administra-
tion of Bush 41, but that was no excuse. Kelley asked
Margaret to quit, and what did she do? She moved out.

Within a year, she was hired away from NY1 by CBS. It
was the big time, national news, and her salary eclipsed Kelley's. Made it look like milk money.

"Daddy!" Ava says. Pounding with the flat of her hand
now, he can tell.

He sighs and opens the door. Ava is pale, and her eyebrows are knitted into a V. Her red hair is tucked behind
her ears, which is exactly how Margaret used to wear it. And
her green eyes, clear as glass, are exactly the same as her
mother's. These eyes are flashing with annoyance now.

"What," Ava asks, "is that *smell?*" She pokes her head
around the door and sees smoke billowing from the bathroom. "What are you *doing,* Daddy?"

"Uh…," he says. He ushers her into the bedroom. He's
afraid if smoke gets in the hallway, the alarms will go off.

She charges like a bull into the bathroom, where she
starts coughing and gagging. "What *is* that?"

"Mitzi's roller disco outfit," he says. "Her headband and her..."

Ava turns on the water in the tub, and the whole mess smokes and hisses like a wet, angry dragon with golden scales.

"...wristbands," Kelley says weakly.

"I saw your Facebook post," she says. "Really, was that necessary?"

"Uh...?" Kelley says. He feels a crushing sense of shame. He is a sixty-two-year-old man who just sought revenge on his wife via social media.

"We are *having* the party tonight," Ava says. She eyeballs the pack of Camels and the bottle of Wild Turkey like a mother superior. "So, please, pull yourself together."

KEVIN

He knows what he has to do. It is only a matter of courage.

And, also, of money. He has socked away twenty-nine thousand dollars in the years since Norah sold their house, took the profit in lieu of alimony payments, and left Nantucket for points south. Twenty-nine grand doesn't sound like a lot, compared with the millions that Patrick makes, but Kevin is pretty proud of himself, considering he gets paid in cash, which could have easily flowed through his hands like water. It takes extreme willpower for him to make it to the bank with a deposit, and yet he does it every week. Before he met Isabelle, he was focused on getting out from under his father's roof—he's thirty-six, and living at the inn has done a number on his self-esteem—but now that he's fallen in love with Isabelle, getting his own place is even *more* important.

He wants to buy a cottage where he can take Isabelle, so the two of them can stop sneaking around. He wants to somehow turn into a man who wears a watch instead of a sailor's bracelet, who owns a nice pair of suede loafers instead of bar clogs, a man who rises at six a.m. to work, rather than at noon.

Is it a winning strategy to spend two or three or five thousand dollars on an engagement ring?

His stomach squelches with nerves.

No more women. It was a vow he made to himself.

It's not just Isabelle, though. There is a baby. He is going to be a father. It's time for actual self-improvement, which will start with bravery, and an abandonment of his bitterness. He can't let his actions now be dictated by what happened with Norah; if he does, then he is *still* letting her control him.

He will spend five thousand dollars on an engagement ring.

Elin Hilderbrand

But.

Kevin is in bed, his cell phone resting on the pillow next to him, which is where Isabelle's head should be. She is in the house somewhere. She and Ava are probably running around trying to get ready for the party tonight without Mitzi. If Kevin sets foot out in the hallway, he will be enlisted to help. Never mind that he brought home cases of beer, wine, liquor, and mixers from the Bar last night. He will be asked to carry things, hang things, move things, and possibly chop and stir things.

He closes his eyes. If he's going to do this, then he has to get into town sooner rather than later. The red-ticket drawing is at three o'clock, and Main Street will be mobbed by one thirty. After the drawing, the Catholics will go to Mass, and everyone else will go drinking until the time comes to descend on the Winter Street Inn, for the biggest open-invitation party on the island.

He's running out of time.

He does what he always does when he feels scared, unsure, adrift: he calls his mother.

"Sweetie?" she says, answering on the first ring. "How are things there?"

"Um...?" Kevin says.

"I know Mitzi left," Margaret says. "I wonder how your dad is doing."

"I haven't seen him since it happened," Kevin says. "I was at work."

"I can't imagine he's taking it well," Margaret says. "He's

70

not good with rejection. And Bart just deployed, and we've lost sixteen soldiers over there in the past forty-eight hours. It must feel like Armageddon there."

"Um...yes? Kind of?" Kevin says. "And Patrick isn't coming home, I guess."

Margaret gasps. "What? Why *not?*"

"I'm not really sure?" Kevin says. Margaret, being a television journalist, asks question after question after question, but Kevin isn't good at disseminating family gossip. That's his sister's department. "You'll have to check with him? Or Ava?"

"I'll do that," Margaret says. He hears her typing on her computer. "And how are *you,* sweetie? What's going on in *your* world?"

"Well," he says, "I have something to tell you."

"Whatever it is, honey, whatever you need, I'm here for you," Margaret says. "You know that, right?"

She's assuming it's bad news — because when, in his adult life, has Kevin ever called with good news?

He blurts it all out in one long stream. It sounds something like, *ImetsomeoneshesFrenchsheworksattheinnIreally loveherMomI'mgoingtoaskhertomarrymeIthinkandguesswhat she'spregnant.*

Margaret screams. With joy, he thinks. She says to her driver, "Raoul! Raoul! I'm going to be a grandmother again! Oh, honey, I'm so thrilled for you! Now, who is it? Is it Isabelle?"

Kevin is confused. His mother does tend to know everything, but how does she know about Isabelle?

"Yes?" he says.

"I met her, briefly, this summer when I was on Nantucket. She answered the door when I stopped by the inn. She is exquisite! She had those long blond braids and that skin, like a milkmaid's, and then I heard her accent and I thought she was from Switzerland—Lausanne, maybe—but she said Montpellier, where I actually did a segment for *60 Minutes,* once upon a time. There was a demonstration against Sarkozy. Montpellier has a large population of North Africans, and there is a fair amount of unrest."

"So, anyway," Kevin says. He wants to get Margaret off the tangent about the sociopolitical climate in Montpellier and back on topic, which is his own very real fear. "I think I'm going to propose."

"Kevin," Margaret says, "I hear doubt in your voice."

"Once bitten, twice shy," he says.

"I understand, darling," Margaret says. "But you're in love?"

He swallows. "Yes."

"You're really, really in love, where you feel like a fool in a good way?"

"Yes."

"Love is always a gamble, honey. Norah Vale got the best of you, but you were incredibly young. I always blamed myself for that. Your father and I had just split, and you moved to a new place. You had to attach to something and make it a permanent part of yourself, and you chose Norah."

"It wasn't your fault," Kevin says. "It was my fault. You and Dad warned me, but I didn't listen."

"You're stronger now. I trust your instincts, and I'm not lying when I tell you that I *felt* something when I met Isabelle. I mean, how many people do I meet in a given week? Fifty? A hundred? And I met Isabelle briefly four months ago…and something about her stuck with me."

"I'm going to buy a ring this afternoon," Kevin says.

"Yes," Margaret says. "If you're going to propose, it's good to have a ring. Now…would it be undermining your manhood if I offered you an early Christmas present in the form of cash to help you pay for it?"

Kevin laughs and fills with an unexpected relief. It's not just the money, although that certainly helps, and it's a surprise, because Margaret doesn't like to give handouts. *I'm your mother, not an ATM.* Kevin is strengthened by Margaret's confidence in him, and her appreciation of Isabelle.

"My manhood can handle it," Kevin says. "Thank you." He exhales the remainder of his anxiety. "I'm going to be a father."

"Darling, I'm over the moon. It's the best Christmas present ever. I'll have Darcy wire you the money as soon as I get to the studio."

His love and respect for his mother combine to form a surge of golden energy, and Kevin jumps out of bed.

"Thanks, Mom!" he says.

"Is it horrible of me to say I hope it's a little girl?" Margaret says. "I adore Paddy's boys — you know I do — but, oh, how I long for a granddaughter."

"Mom," Kevin says, "absolutely nobody knows about this. Nobody even knows that Isabelle and I are seeing each other. It's going to come as kind of a shock, especially to Dad and Ava, and so I have to beg you to *please* not say anything."

Margaret laughs. She says, "Of course not, honey. What do you think I'm going to do? Announce it on the evening news?"

Oh boy, Kevin thinks. "I love you, Mom," he says.

"Merry Christmas, sweetie," Margaret says. "Good luck!"

AVA

She can't remember ever being *this stressed out.*

It's two o'clock. People are coming in five hours, and Ava has fires to put out everywhere she turns.

Including an *actual fire* in her father's bathtub. He set Mitzi's roller disco outfit ablaze, complete with headband and wristbands. He was in his bedroom, drinking Wild

Turkey and smoking Camels and posting ungenerous things about Mitzi on Facebook. He is probably experiencing some kind of temporary insanity. Once Ava doused the fire and cleared the smoke, she confiscated the whiskey and the cigarettes—and then she yelled at Kelley as if she were his mother, or her own mother, at which point Kelley collapsed on the bed, blubbering about Mitzi and George, and then about Bart. Bart was going to die, Mitzi had seen it in her crystals, Mitzi had told Kelley, but he hadn't listened, he hadn't believed in the crystal reading, but now, he saw she was right: Bart was going to die. Four soldiers had been killed the day before.

Ava still hadn't heard back from Bart, and her breath caught for a second. She didn't mention this to her father; the last thing she wanted to do was upset him further. But she also didn't have time to act as Kelley's therapist. The best she could do was to pull the shades, bring him a glass of ice water, and tuck him into bed for a nap.

He moaned. "Mitzi's gone! Her Mrs. Claus dress is hanging in the closet. Take it away, please. We have no Mrs. Claus and no Santa! How can you think about throwing the party without a Santa?"

"I'll find someone," Ava said. She grabbed Mitzi's red dress out of the closet; it was cruel of her to leave it behind. "You know what I'm going to do, Daddy? I'm going to cook a standing rib roast for dinner tomorrow night. And use the pan drippings for Yorkshire pudding."

Kelley's expression perked up a little. "You are?"

"I am," she said, and they shared a moment of glee, thinking about how beef would be cooked at the Winter Street Inn for the first time since they've owned it.

Mitzi's leaving isn't *all* bad.

Ava took the computer with her when she left the room. Her first order of business was to remedy the Facebook page. The party is on.

Now, she has forty dozen appetizers to prepare—not including dips, not including the cheese board, complete with the salted-almond pinecone. A photograph of the salted-almond pinecone was once featured on the cover of *Nantucket* magazine, and it instantly became a holiday icon. Now, everyone has come to expect it.

Isabelle is helping Ava, but every twenty or thirty minutes, she excuses herself for the bathroom, and once she is gone for so long that Ava goes to check on her, fearing she has walked out (could Ava blame her?), and she hears Isabelle puking in the bathroom. When Isabelle emerges, Ava says, "Are you sick?"

"No, no, no," Isabelle says. But her normally rosy cheeks are ashen, and she's perspiring.

"You were vomiting," Ava says.

"Something I eat," Isabelle says. "Sushi. From the supermarket."

"Ew," Ava says. She has to say, she will be relieved if it's food poisoning. The last thing they need is a stomach bug that would systematically mow down the household. That happened once, on Easter a few years back, and since then, Ava hasn't been able to look at a leg of lamb without wincing....

"Do you want to lie down?" Ava asks worriedly. "If you're not feeling well?"

"No, no!" Isabelle says. "I'm fine!"

But she doesn't look fine, and her insistence that she *is* fine makes Ava think there might be something else going on.

Pregnant? she wonders.

But despite the fact that Isabelle is pretty and sweet and has an indescribable allure common to many Frenchwomen, she has no boyfriend. She doesn't ever date — probably because she has no time. She spends every waking hour at the inn.

Then, Ava gets an idea.

The list of things they must accomplish by seven o'clock is long. Hurry hurry hurry. There's the Christmas Eve party for 150 guests tonight, and Christmas dinner tomorrow. Ava calls to order a standing rib roast. Yes, they have one left, which they can reserve for her. She can come pick it up anytime. That's good!

But Patrick is mysteriously not coming home, Mitzi has left with George, her father is losing his mind, and now Isabelle is under the weather due to supermarket sushi. How does Ava possibly have a second to think about Nathaniel?

She doesn't. And yet she thinks about him nonstop, like a stuck note on a piano, E-flat, her least-favorite note.

He called her twice from the road yesterday. But no messages and no text saying he arrived safely, which is a rule they've established whenever one of them travels. She must have pissed him off by not answering? Possibly lost him forever, when all she was trying to do was seem elusive? It's nearly impossible for Ava to seem elusive when her life is so prescribed—school day from eight a.m. to three p.m., and then, over the Christmas holidays, she is chained to the inn.

She doesn't break down and call him until three o'clock, when she hides in her bedroom. Outside, the sun is getting ready to set.

Nathaniel doesn't answer his phone, and Ava knows this is exactly what she deserves. She has never been good at playing hard to get—it always backfires—and yet playing easy to get, which has been her strategy from the start, hasn't worked either. She and Nathaniel have been dating for nearly two years, and there has been no mention of getting married or cohabitating, or even of taking a vacation together, although this is primarily because Nathaniel has no money, and, really, neither does Ava. Their level of commitment is stuck at a six out of ten—this is how Ava thinks of it—with occasional jumps to seven or eight (her birthday in July, when he took her to Topper's at the Wauwinet and gave her a card that said, *I love you, Ava Quinn*) and occasional setbacks to five or four (like right now—no communication for twenty-two hours, no text saying, *Got here safely, missing you!*)

It's not fair! Ava's ardor for Nathaniel has been cranked to a ten out of ten since the day she met him. He showed up at the Winter Street Inn one day the spring before last to build Mitzi a set of pantry doors. And not just any pantry doors — Mitzi wanted mahogany inlay and a fancy cutout featuring wooden forks and spoons. She had seen similar pantry doors at her friend Kai the Massage Therapist's house, and Kai had put Mitzi in touch with Nathaniel Oscar, maker of fancy and special pantry doors.

Ava had been the one to answer the door when Nathaniel knocked. For her, it was love at first sight. He wore jeans and a tool belt and a pressed red-and-white striped oxford shirt and a red fleece vest and a faded red visor from Cisco Brewers. When Ava opened the door, he was clenching a pencil between his teeth, which he dropped expertly into his hand so that he could flash a smile at Ava.

"Hi," he said. "I'm Nathaniel. Are you Mitzi?"

Ava had laughed at that. "I'm *Ava!*" she said. "Ava Quinn?" She thought the name might resonate with him. The Quinn family was pretty famous on Nantucket — because they owned the Winter Street Inn, because they threw the huge Christmas Eve party, because Ava taught school and knew everybody, and Kevin worked at the Bar and knew everybody else, because Bart was in the police blotter two or three times a year for screwing up in spectacular ways, and because they were all related to Margaret Quinn of the CBS *Evening News*. But Nathaniel just smiled. Ava Quinn was just another pretty girl who opened the door to him and swooned.

She led him to the kitchen and showed him the doorless pantry in question and asked him if he wanted a glass of water or a Coke or a beer.

He lit right up. "I'd love a beer. But only if you'll join me."

Ava opened two Whale's Tales, and then Nathaniel got to work measuring. Ava felt like an idiot just standing around watching him, so she took her beer to the next room and started playing Chopin on the piano. Chopin was show-offy, perfect when trying to make a first impression. She then switched to Beethoven's "Für Elise," which he would recognize if he had an ounce of culture at all, and then she sailed into Schubert's Impromptu in G-flat. By the time she finished, she was perspiring, and Nathaniel was standing in the doorway, wide-eyed with awe.

"Wow," he said. "You can really play! And the Impromptu is my favorite."

And Ava thought, *Did he really just say that?*

Yes: Nathaniel Oscar, maker of fancy and special pantry doors, was born an aristocrat. He grew up in a family manse on Clapboard Ridge Road in Greenwich, Connecticut, he attended Greenwich Country Day School, then St. George's, in Newport, then Brown University, then Duke Law School. But the summer before he was to start a job with Sullivan &

Cromwell LLP, he visited Nantucket and decided he never wanted to leave. He apprenticed himself to a genius woodworker named Paul Pitcher, and when Paul died suddenly of a brain aneurysm, Nathaniel took over his business. Paul Pitcher used to listen to classical music in the workshop, Nathaniel said, and the habit stuck.

Nathaniel loved old things, fine things; he used salvaged materials whenever he could. His work was refined and elegant; it was pedigreed and expensive. When Nathaniel delivered the bill for the fancy and special pantry doors, Kelley hollered. But by then, Ava and Nathaniel were dating, and the rest of the family was half in love with him as well. When Margaret visited Nantucket in August, she took Ava and Nathaniel to American Seasons for dinner. Nathaniel told Margaret about spending his junior year abroad in Gambia, where he dug wells and implemented clean-water programs, and Margaret was smitten.

Marry him! she told Ava.

And Ava said, *I'm trying!*

She had lured Nathaniel in with her piano playing and then got him even closer with her stories of the kids at school. He loved kids, although he didn't seem to be in any hurry for his own. But somewhere along the way, they stalled, or Ava did. She doesn't remember anything going wrong, and they never fought — mostly because Ava tried really, really hard to be agreeable — but after they had been dating eight or nine months, Ava noticed Nathaniel seeking a little more personal space. He went out some nights with guys on his crew, he took a Greyhound bus trip to Seattle to see "friends from prep school," and there was no mention of Ava flying out to meet him. And then, in October, he told Ava about his reconnection with the dreaded Kirsten Cabot, which corresponded exactly with Kirsten's impending divorce from a friend of Nathaniel's named Bimal, who was Indian, had a British accent, was fantastically wealthy, and was a very nice guy besides, according to Nathaniel. Ava wished that Nathaniel had reconnected with Bimal instead of Kirsten, although she wasn't at all surprised that Kirsten had reached out to Nathaniel. Nathaniel was the One Who Got Away to every one of his ex-girlfriends. What could be more romantic than a man who had eschewed corporate law for a life doing custom woodwork on Nantucket Island?

Ava told herself not to feel jealous of Kirsten Cabot. After all, Nathaniel was up front about the reconnection on Facebook; it wasn't like he was hiding anything. Ava, however, found herself stalking Kirsten Cabot on Facebook and Twitter. Kirsten owned an upscale clothing boutique in Greenwich Village called Choice, and Ava visited the Choice Facebook page and even "liked" it. There were photos of Kirsten on the Facebook page, and in every single one, she looked beautiful. Ava spent long minutes staring at the photos, enlarging them, minimizing them, trying to make Kirsten look less beautiful. Wasn't her smile too wide, too toothy? Wasn't her ass a little square? No, that wasn't a winning strategy—Kirsten was drop-dead gorgeous, stunning, a knockout. She was the kind of woman men stared at, turned their heads for. Hot.

At that moment, Ava's cell phone rings. The screen says NO.

It's Nathaniel.

NO, she thinks. She shouldn't answer.

But she just called him. She can't pretend that she's now suddenly unavailable.

"Hello?" she says.

"Ava?"

"Uh-huh?"

"Did you call?"

"Yes," she says. "I wanted to make sure you made it there safely."

"Oh," he says. "Yeah, of course I did."

"Okay," she says.

Long pause.

He says, "So, how's your holiday?"

Where to begin? The stark truth overwhelms her. To tell him about her family quite literally *falling apart* will be such a turnoff, he might never come back to her. She wants to tell him something happy, something fabulous.

"I'm headed to the airport," she says.

"You *are?*" he says.

"I'm flying to Boston," Ava says. "And then my mom is taking me to Maui for a few days."

Throat clearing. He gets flustered any time he remembers she is Margaret Quinn's daughter.

"When did this come about?" he asks.

"This morning," Ava says. "We're staying at the Four Seasons."

"You *are?*" he says. "When are you coming back?"

"Next week sometime?" she says. "I can't remember, exactly."

"Oh," he says, and she knows that, somehow, she's reached him. She says, "What are *you* doing?"

"We're headed to the Cabots' for cocktails," he says.

Ava takes a second to digest this, then feels like she's been one-upped. She *has* been one-upped, of course, because she's *not* headed to the Four Seasons in Maui with her famous mother. She is headed back to the Winter Street Inn kitchen to make the salted-almond pinecone. And later, she will be banging out "Jingle Bells" on the piano while 150 voices sing along off-key, making Ava want to cry.

She is stuck here, like a partridge in a flipping pear tree.

"What's going on at the Cabots'?" she asks.

"Kirsten's parents have a little cocktail thing every year. It's lots of drinking, basically, and then we order pizza and cheesesteaks from the Pizza Post. Same since I was a kid."

"I can relate," Ava says. She wonders how many people will complain because there is no punch bowl with Mitzi's god-awful Cider of a Thousand Cloves.

"I should be home by eight," Nathaniel says. "Definitely by nine. I'll call you. What time do you take off?"

"Take off?" she says.

"Your flight."

"Oh. Midnight, I think?"

"All right," he says. "I'll call before you leave."

"Will you?" she says, hating how desperate she sounds. "Do you *promise?*"

"Yes, baby," he says. "Of course I promise." His voice is tender, and for a second it's like the best of times; it's an eight or a nine.

"Okay," Ava says. "Bye-bye." And she hangs up before anything can change.

KELLEY

When Kelley wakes from his nap, he sends a text to Bart's cell phone. The text says: *Mommy and I are splitting.*

No mention of why. In this, Kelley feels he's being generous.

Kelley is informed by his phone that the message is undeliverable.

PATRICK

G<small>ARY</small> Grimstead, Great Guy, says: *Compliance had no choice, baby, and now the SEC is involved, and they're seeing* something *they don't like. Anything you want to tell me? If you tell me now, if you come clean, it will be better. Trust me, baby.*

Gary Grimstead always uses the diminutive "baby"; he fancies himself an incarnation of Vince Vaughn's character in *Swingers*. Patrick has never liked being called "baby" by someone who is actually eleven months younger than him and who went to an inferior college and business school and yet is his boss. But Gary Grimstead is one of those magnetic people everyone loves and falls over themselves to please. Gary has never lorded his authority over Patrick; he treats Patrick like an equal. They are friends who golf together and sit together in the corporate suite at Red Sox games, bonded by the fact that they both hate the Sox. Patrick grew up a Yankees fan, and Gary likes the Angels. Patrick knows Gary has Patrick's best interests at heart, but, even so, it feels dangerous to tell him the truth. Can he say the words out loud?

"The *SEC?*" Patrick says, his tone conveying the maximum amount of incredulity. "Because of the *perks?* I can see Compliance giving me a slap on the wrist, telling me I have to be more judicious about who I accept favors from, but it's an industry-wide pathology, Gary. I mean, I'm hardly the only private-equity guy on the East Coast taking perks."

"It's not the perks," Gary says. "It's the amount you invested with Panagea. It's a lot of money, baby. It sent up a red flag. They're looking into all your shit. Now, is there anything you want to tell me?"

"Panagea is a gamble," Patrick says. "That's what we do in this business. We gamble."

"So, here's the thing. Panagea has had nothing going on for years; I mean, how long has their stock been at twelve dollars? I'll tell you how long—since October 2006. Then, all of a sudden, out of nowhere, you pour twenty-five mil into this company? And you think nobody's going to notice?"

You didn't notice, Patrick thinks.

"I've been reading their R and D reports for years," Patrick says. "I've always had a feeling about them. You know I always go with my gut."

"They have a new drug," Gary says. "MDP. Cures leukemia in kids. That's no secret."

Patrick holds his breath. He simply doesn't know how much to admit to.

"Twenty-five point six million is a hell of a gamble," Gary says. "If that leukemia drug isn't FDA approved, you're sunk. If the drug *is* approved, it looks like you know something. Do you know something?"

"No," Patrick says, but his voice gives him away. He

sounds too defensive. "So, how was the party? You didn't do any Irish car bombs without me, did you?"

"Patrick," Gary says. "This is serious. My ass is on the line, too, baby. Tell me what's going on."

Tell him, Patrick thinks. Gary's ass *is* on the line. He won't go to jail, but he might lose his job. Patrick sinks to the kitchen floor and rests his elbows on his knees, one hand grabbing a hank of hair, pulling until it really hurts. What has he *done?* What should he *do?*

Deny, deny, deny, he thinks. If he tells the truth, he's cooked. If he continues to lie, there is still hope. They can't prove anything.

"Nothing is going on," Patrick says. "They can look, but I'm clean, man. And, seeing as it's Christmas Eve, I should go. I'm taking the family to church."

On the other end, Gary is quiet.

Patrick says, "Man, I'm serious. I'm clean."

Gary says, "Okay, baby, I hope so. I really do. Merry Christmas."

Patrick inhales all eight eggs and half the caviar; then he feels queasy. He is now not only a cheat but also a liar. He hurries down the hall to the master bedroom; he's going to be sick. He stands over the sink and presses his forehead against the bathroom mirror. They won't catch him; they can't prove anything. Then he thinks, *Of course they'll catch me. They catch everyone.*

The Boston bombers got caught in four days.

Twenty-five point six million. If the drug is approved, this number will hit the stratosphere. Patrick was tripped up by greed. It's a deadly sin; now he knows why. He sees the bottle of Vicodin—ten pills left. Would ten Vicodin be enough to kill him?

He's too much of a chicken to kill himself. He loves life, he loves Jen and the kids, he loves this house, the city of Boston, the Commonwealth of Massachusetts; he loves America.

He throws some clothes and his Dopp kit in a duffel bag and goes out to the living room. The tree is a sparkling wonder; the entire month of December, people have been gathering on the sidewalk below to point and gaze. And it smells good—rich and piney. It pains Patrick to turn the lights off, but he has no choice.

He is going to Nantucket.

MARGARET

Ten more soldiers killed in Afghanistan. Margaret is breathless with horror, followed by shame. She has been anchoring the national news for over twenty years, she has reported on thousands of deaths of American soldiers, and yet it is only this week, now that her children's brother has been deployed, that she truly understands how scary and dangerous it is. The sacrifice these kids make (and they are kids—Bart is only nineteen; the last time Margaret saw him, eighteen months earlier, he was in New York City on his senior class trip) is astonishing—as are the sacrifices the parents make, sending their sons and daughters into battle. The parents. Kelley and Mitzi.

"I'm behind on Afghanistan," Margaret admits to her assistant, Darcy, who is, on any given day, one of the most informed people at the network. "Why all these deaths all of a sudden? Can you explain it?"

"The U.S. wanted to have the majority of their troops withdrawn by year's end," Darcy says. "They've been pulling out far more troops than they're sending in. And insurgent forces know this. With fewer U.S. troops, it's safer for Afghan nationals who support the Taliban to make their presence known. They're striking out left and right. Quite frankly, I'd be surprised if they don't attempt a full-on takeover." Darcy pushes her glasses higher on her nose. "I'd say Afghanistan is more dangerous now than it ever has been."

"Well, great," Margaret says. "Bart Quinn just got shipped over."

"Yes, you told me," Darcy says. "He isn't...on the list, is he?"

Margaret scans the list. "No, thank God." *Not today,* she thinks.

"Can you imagine the parents who are getting the news…
on Christmas Eve?" Darcy says.

Margaret thinks about those parents, and something
unusual happens. She tears up. She hasn't cried over the
news since she famously broke down on the air when the
first tower collapsed on September 11. Initially, she received
all kinds of criticism for losing her composure. But Margaret
thinks—actually, she knows—that it was her coverage on
September 11 that caught the attention of the big boss, Lee
Kramer, and launched her into the evening anchor spot.

Margaret wipes at her eyes with the back of her hand,
and Darcy silently retreats.

Margaret's cell phone rings.

Drake, she thinks, *canceling.*

But it's Ava.

"Darling!" Margaret says.

"Mommy," Ava says.

"Darling, what is it?" Margaret checks her computer: it's
quarter to five. She's due in Wardrobe in fifteen minutes.
Red tonight, for sure, which will make her wish she had a
bag over her head; the Nasty Blogger, Queenie229, will have
a field day. What would be happening in Ava's world at
quarter to five on Christmas Eve?

"I want to come to Hawaii with you," Ava says in a small
voice. It is a voice from the past, her little-girl voice, and
instinctively Margaret fills with guilt. *I want to come with
you, Mommy.* This was Ava, every afternoon when Margaret

was getting ready to head to the studio. *I want you. I can't stop wanting you.* Ava would cry, and Margaret would have to peel Ava off her, and hand her over to Lotus, the housekeeper-nanny. Oh, the guilt! Ava would be home from school for only five minutes before Margaret had to go to work. In the days when she was at NY1, she saw the kids for an average of two hours during the week, and then she tried to make it all up to them on the weekends—but some weekends she was called in to work, too. It doesn't really matter that Margaret is now sitting on the golden throne of broadcast journalism; she missed so much of her kids' lives growing up, it tears her apart.

She missed so much.

"Hawaii?" Margaret says. "Oh, honey."

"Did you not mean it when you invited me?" Ava says. "I really, *really* want to get out of here."

"I'm going to Hawaii with my friend Drake," Margaret says. "When I asked you, I was serious that I wanted you to come, but I was also kidding because we didn't arrange it. I would love to take you to Hawaii, sweetheart. We'll plan it for next year, I promise. Would you like to come with me next year?"

"Next year?" Ava says.

"I never thought you would want to leave the island during the holidays," Margaret says. "It's such a big deal for you—the inn, the party; I never thought you would seriously consider coming with me, honey. Otherwise I would have asked you in September, when I booked it."

"So there's no way I can go?" Ava asks. "Who's Drake?"

"You met Drake," Margaret says. "Once, on Nantucket. He stayed overnight with me at the White Elephant? He's the pediatric brain surgeon...?" Margaret's voice falters. She doesn't want Ava to think that she would rather be with some on-again, off-again boyfriend than her own daughter. But to cancel with Drake at this point would be cruel. "What's really bothering you, sweetheart? Is it Daddy?"

"Yes, it's Daddy!" Ava says. "He nearly burned the house down, setting Mitzi's roller disco outfit on fire!"

Oh my, Margaret thinks.

"He's smoking cigarettes and drinking whiskey and posting toxic things about Mitzi on Facebook. Meanwhile, the party is in two hours and Daddy hasn't lifted a finger and Kevin is missing and Patrick isn't coming home, so who gets stuck holding the bag? Me!"

"Oh, sweetie," Margaret says. She's a woman with a comprehensive vocabulary, but that is all she can come up with to say. She is thinking of herself and Kelley at a certain bar in the Village, drinking beer and doing shots, smoking cigarettes, Margaret in jeans and a black turtleneck, Kelley in a fisherman's sweater; after they played Traffic on the jukebox and paid the bill, they had enough money to split a grilled cheese sandwich at the Greek diner. More tears: what is *wrong* with her? She remembers that Margaret and that Kelley, that *couple,* so fondly, like they are dear friends she hasn't seen in a long time. They were the happiest people she knew.

They didn't need big careers or their own brownstone or piles of money.

"Poor Daddy," Margaret says. Mitzi has gone and broken Kelley's heart — although Margaret knows that she broke it first and she broke it best.

"And that's not even my real problem," Ava says.

"What *is* your real problem?" Margaret asks. "Tell me."

"It's a long story," Ava says. "And you must have to go soon?"

It's five minutes to five. Darcy has suddenly reappeared, indicating that it's nearly time for Wardrobe and Makeup.

"Please tell me, darling," Margaret says.

"Nathaniel is in Greenwich, Connecticut, with his family," Ava says. "His beautiful ex-girlfriend who just got divorced is also there. I'm scared and I'm jealous and I'm lonely. I got on the phone with him and told him I was going to Hawaii with you. I want him to think I'm fabulous, I want to be elusive, I want him to propose, but I'm a straight fail across the board."

"Ava," Margaret says, in her serious Mom voice, "you are not a fail."

"Yes," Ava says, "I am."

"I love you, Ava."

"I love you, too, Mommy. Have fun in Hawaii." With that, Ava hangs up. Margaret holds the phone for a second. Then, not knowing what else to do, she heads down the hall — toward Wardrobe and the red dress.

AVA

Scott Skyler arrives at six o'clock, and Ava hands him the Santa suit.

"You're about half the size of George," Ava says. "I really don't think this is going to fit you."

"I'll make it work," Scott says. "Don't worry."

"You're a lifesaver and a saint," Ava says. "I don't know why you always come to the rescue."

"Don't you?" Scott says, and he gives Ava a searing *I want you* look. He has given Ava this look three or four times before, the first time several years earlier, while sitting at the bar at Lola 41. Ava had been out with her girlfriend Shelby, the school librarian, but Shelby left to pick up her teenage sons, and so Ava was sitting alone when Scott wandered in. He told her he had just been promoted from fifth-grade teacher to assistant principal. This came as such surprising news (elementary schools are petri dishes of gossip; Ava couldn't believe she hadn't heard any rumor of the promotion) that Ava threw her arms around Scott's neck and kissed his cheek.

"I'm so *proud* of you!" she said. She was three drinks into the night and as such was overly animated. She was also struck by the novelty of seeing *Scott Skyler* at Lola. Lola was a dark, sexy place that served sushi and ruby red grapefruit martinis; it was a place where Ava normally ran into the divorced parents of her students, not Scott Skyler.

"Thanks," Scott said. He was a tall guy with superhero shoulders, and that night he'd seemed even taller. He eschewed his usual Budweiser and ordered something called a Poison Dragonfly—and by the time he was at the end of his drink, he was narrowing his eyes in desire at Ava, telling her he was in love with her. He'd been in love with her since the first time he saw her play the piano at school assembly. *And even before that!* he said. Because he'd attended the Christmas Eve party at the Winter Street Inn with his older sister years earlier, and he'd seen Ava ladling out the Cider of a Thousand Cloves and thought she was the most beautiful creature alive.

Ava scoffed. She thought, *The Poison Dragonfly has created a master of hyperbole!* She was *not* the most beautiful creature alive, not by a long shot. She was, like her mother, handsome—or she would be handsome, she supposed, when she got older.

Now Scott is giving her the fired-up look again, and Ava thinks he might try to kiss her. She surreptitiously looks up to make sure she isn't standing under any mistletoe.

She says to him, "You're a good egg for coming, Scottie." She pats him on the shoulder.

He gets it. His face settles into resignation; it's territory they have covered before. Ava doesn't reciprocate his feelings. It's not that she doesn't *want* to—she does! She likes him and loves him, she admires him, she thinks he is the owner of a golden heart and an incorruptible character and a solid intellect. He is tall and strong and handsome; he has nice, thick hair, and he looks good in cable-knit sweaters. When he's using his Assistant Principal Skyler voice, he can silence an auditorium filled with kids; it's pretty impressive.

But with Scott there isn't any spark, any juice; that one salient, mysterious ingredient is missing.

"Have you heard from Nathaniel?" Scott asks.

Ava nods. "I broke down and called him." She pauses, wondering if she should confess that she lied about going to Hawaii and then tried to make it a not-lie by calling Margaret, only to find out that her mother has a doctor named Drake joining her in Hawaii, and, even if she didn't, it would be really expensive and impractical to include Ava at the last minute.

Ava decides that Scott doesn't need to know all this. She doesn't want him to know that she's resorted to lying to hold on to Nathaniel. "Nathaniel is going over to what's-her-name's house. I guess the parents have this cocktail thingy. He said he'll call me later. Eight or nine."

Scott gives her a penetrating look that lasts just long enough to throw Ava into self-doubt.

"I'll go put on the suit," he says.

And then, Ava remembers her idea!

She has never set anyone up in her life; she knows nothing about it. There used to be a matchmaker on Nantucket named Dabney Kimball Beech. Dabney had been the closest thing Nantucket had to a local celebrity, but she succumbed to cancer in the fall. Dabney set up Ava's friend Shelby with her husband, Zack, which practically makes Shelby famous—not to mention lucky. Dabney's matches always stay happily married.

Ava decides to channel the spirit of Dabney Kimball Beech and try her hand at matchmaking. She finds Mitzi's sexy Mrs. Claus dress and presents it to Isabelle.

"Would you mind wearing this tonight?" Ava asks.

Isabelle looks confused. *"Ce soir?"*

"You can be Mrs. Claus," Ava says. "You'll help Scott with the children. All you have to do is keep them in line and then take the photos."

Isabelle seems unsure.

"Are you feeling better now?" Ava asks.

Isabelle nods decisively.

"Great!" Ava says. "Just put on the dress and some black shoes. I'll show you what to do. It'll be fun!"

Ava then goes to check on things in the kitchen. The salted-almond pinecone is done, as are the cheese board, the smoked salmon dip, the hot sausage dip, the sugared dates stuffed with peanut butter, the red, green, and white crudité tray, and the tea sandwiches. Isabelle has already pre-heated the oven, and she lined up the hors d'oeuvres on hotel pans.

Kevin set up the bar the night before, and he went out to get ice a while ago, but it's taking him a long time. In general, Ava would say that she feels almost completely abandoned: Her mother is going to Hawaii with a doctor named Drake (he sounds like a character from a soap opera), Patrick is...? Kevin is...? Bart is...in Afghanistan somewhere? Nathaniel is on his way to Kirsten Cabot's house. Her father is locked in his bedroom. And Mitzi is...? Ava wouldn't have thought herself capable of missing Mitzi, but, oddly, as Ava stands in the warm kitchen, listening to the *Nutcracker* Suite playing on the whole-inn sound system, the person she misses is Mitzi. Ava's relationship with Mitzi was troubled from the start; it's safe to say that Ava tolerated Mitzi on a good day and was openly hostile on a bad day. But this is Mitzi's party, and in years past, Mitzi has made it sparkle with her own irrepressible Christmas spirit. She wore the Mrs. Claus suit, she sang along loudest to the carols, and her enthusiasm, although at times over-the-top, was contagious.

In years past, this party was the closest Ava came to the true Christmas spirit of her youth. Nantucket Island, by anyone's standards, is a wonderland at the holidays. Ava remembers her first Christmas here. She and her father had gone into town alone to shop for last-minute presents. It was dark at four thirty in the afternoon, and Ava had stood at the base of Main Street, marveling at the trees, with their colored lights running up either side of the street all the way to Pacific National Bank, where the giant tree with its 1609 white fairy lights twinkled. The shopwindows were decorated with evergreen boughs, candy canes, and blown-glass ornaments. Her father bought her a hot chocolate with one pillowy, homemade marshmallow that left powdered sugar on her lip—and then on his lip too, when she kissed him to say thank you. They had bought Patrick and Kevin neckties from Murray's—which they would be expected to wear to Mass—and then, with her own allowance, Ava had bought their dog at the time, Lucy, a new collar and a bag of rawhides. As Ava and Kelley walked home, they sang carols. First, Ava's favorite, "Angels We Have Heard on High," and then Kelley's favorite, "Silent Night."

Ava wanders out to the living room now and tries to feel the emotions she felt then. The tree is a Christmas narrative unto itself because of the ornaments Mitzi has collected. Growing up, Mitzi's mother was part of a Christmas club, where all the women made ornaments to exchange. There is a mama hedgehog made from a thistle, a baby mouse nestled in half a walnut shell, and a Santa made from a hollowed-out egg. Some of the ornaments are over forty years old; Mitzi has taken excellent care of them. When Ava was younger, she was fascinated by the stories behind the ornaments— there's a reindeer face crafted out of the nipple of a baby bottle that Mrs. Wilson made in honor of Mrs. Glass the year Mrs. Glass gave birth to triplets. There is a stuffed felt Snoopy with paper-clip ice skates made by Mrs. Simon, who was Jewish but who wanted to be included in the Christmas Club anyway. In later years, other ornaments were added— there is a surfboard for Kevin, skis for Patrick, a tiny piano that plays—*sigh*...—"Jingle Bells" for Ava. There is a papier-mâché roller skate that Kelley got for Mitzi their first Christmas together.

Ava inhales the scent of fragrant evergreen; then she studies the nutcrackers—the scuba diver is her first favorite, followed by the fisherman. She admires the silver bowls of enormous pinecones that Mitzi buys every year from a fir farm in Colorado, and the glass apothecary jars filled with ribbon candy. There are birch logs stacked neatly in the fireplace. The room is more Christmassy than the North Pole. Why isn't this working?

Well, as Mitzi herself has long said, what makes a tradition special is who you share it with.

Scott steps out of the powder room in the suit and a white wig and beard. "How do I look?" he asks.

Before Ava can comment—he needs help straightening his beard—the doorbell rings.

Ava panics. It's six thirty. There have indeed been years when guests have appeared early—but not this early. *And, please, not this year.* Ava isn't even dressed. This year, she bought a black velvet cocktail dress, thinking Nathaniel might propose and she might possibly be the center of attention.

She goes to the front door, Scott trailing behind her. "No early birds," she says to Scott. "You'll back me up?"

"Always," he says.

Ava swings open the big oak door to see a portly, white-haired man in a flannel shirt and an unzipped parka.

"Ava," he says.

It takes her a minute.

It's George. George the Santa Claus.

Ava opens her mouth, but no sound comes out. She feels Scott standing right behind her, and she watches George take in the sight of Scott in his Santa suit. Ava feels an apology forming in her mind; then she thinks, *No!* She does not owe George an apology.

"What..." she says, "can I do for you?"

"Is your father at home?" George asks. "I'd like to speak to him, man-to-man."

"Uh...," she says. Ava is thrown by the phrase "man-to-man." Is there another way they would speak to each other? She hates herself for floundering. But really, it's unfair that she alone has been left to navigate the emotional land mines this family has created for itself.

Suddenly, Isabelle appears out of nowhere. "*Bon soir,* George," she says. "Come in, please? I will get monsieur."

Ava can't decide if she should feel angered or relieved by Isabelle's intervening. She chooses relieved. She and Scott/Santa step aside so that George can enter.

George says to Scott, "You look good in the suit."

Scott says, "I'm a big guy, but I have to say, I'm glad this came with a belt."

Ava bites her tongue to keep from laughing. Scott is her hero.

Isabelle vanishes into the owners' quarters, and Ava notices an awkward silence between George the Old Santa Claus and Scott the New Santa Claus.

George says, "Place looks great." He eyes the mantel. "There are the nutcrackers. I have to say, I always enjoyed looking at them. I'm fond of the bagpiper."

"Scuba diver," Ava says.

Scott says, "Hmm...I'm partial to the pirate."

George scans the rest of the room. "So, you must be getting ready."

There is genuine rue and longing in his voice, and Ava realizes that George is going to miss being at the party. He is going to *miss* being Santa. He is, probably, very jealous of Scott right now. He is, probably, assuaging his jealousy by thinking that, being a portly man, he is a much more natural-looking Santa.

After a long, long moment, during which Ava takes only six metered breaths, Kevin bursts in from the back, holding an Igloo boat cooler full of ice.

He says, "The iceman cometh!" with a hilarious grin. He takes in the sight of George and Ava and Scott dressed as Santa with his usual equanimity. "Hey, George."

"Kevin," George says.

Kevin takes the cooler to the back corner of the room, where he starts to set up the bar, whistling. *Oh, to be Kevin,* Ava thinks. Happy and oblivious.

Isabelle emerges from the owners' quarters. "Monsieur says you can go back."

Everyone seems shocked by this pronouncement. Ava's roommate at Berklee College of Music was an opera singer, and when she became, in her words, *verklempt,* she would sing the highest note in her range. Ava hears the note now, in her head; it's shrill enough to break glass or summon every dog in the neighborhood.

George clears his throat. "Back...?"

"To *sa chambre,*" Isabelle says. "His room? You do know where it is, *n'est-ce pas?*"

Despite the fact that English is her second language, there is unmistakable innuendo in Isabelle's voice, and Ava feels a surge of admiration. Isabelle has just proven herself to be on *their* side, even though it was Mitzi who brought her into the fold.

"Yes," George says, "I think so." He tugs at the bottom of his flannel shirt and heads down the hallway. Ava, Scott, Isabelle, and Kevin watch him go.

"Tequila shot, anyone?" Kevin asks.

KELLEY

He's not entirely sober, and the room still reeks of smoke when George knocks, but this does not derail Kelley from his mission. As soon as the door opens, Kelley punches George in the mouth as hard as he can. The punch lands squarely, with the solid, satisfying noise of flesh on flesh.

When was the last time Kelley *hit* someone? He comes up with a party at the Alpha Chi Rho house at Gettysburg his junior year; a brawl broke out over the honor of someone's date, who, it was later disclosed, wasn't very honorable at all. Punching another man in the face, especially sucker punching someone who isn't expecting it, isn't exactly honorable either, but to Kelley it feels good, just, and right.

George's head snaps back, and blood gushes everywhere. George moans and spits out a tooth. Kelley feels delighted, as if a stream of quarters were flying from his slot machine.

George makes no move to retaliate. "I guess I deserved that."

"Oh God, yes," Kelley says. "At least that."

George pulls a handkerchief out of his pocket and wipes up the spittle and blood. His eyes are out of focus, which pleases Kelley further; he really walloped the guy.

Twelve years! Kelley thinks.

"Can I come in and talk to you, please?" George asks.

Kelley steps out of the way, ushering George in and closing the door behind him.

If it's awkward to have this conversation in the bedroom that Kelley and Mitzi shared for so many years, neither man acknowledges it. Kelley sits on the edge of the bed while George stands before him. Kelley is dizzy and has the beginnings of a hangover; all he wants is a drink to take the edge off his drinking binge.

"Do you have a flask?" Kelley asks George.

"Actually," George says, "I do." He pulls a leather flask—monogrammed, no less—out of the pocket of his parka and hands it to Kelley.

Kelley accepts it with glee and something that feels like love. For a fleeting instant, he understands what Mitzi sees in George. He takes a swig—Johnnie Walker Black. Brilliant! Kelley hands the flask to George, who takes a slug, and then George hands it back to Kelley. George is a good and generous man.

"I came to say I'm sorry," George says.

"Sorry doesn't begin to address it," Kelley says. He takes another drink, savoring the burn down his throat. "You've been sleeping with my wife for twelve years. Is that true? Is that *true,* George?"

"Saying 'twelve years' makes it sound worse than it is," George says. He dabs his handkerchief at his swollen lip. "It was a few times every year at Christmas. It was a holiday thing."

"It was a *holiday thing?*" Kelley says. Did George really

just say that sleeping with Kelley's wife was a *holiday thing*—like caroling or baking gingerbread?

"It just happened," George says. "Do you remember twelve years ago, when the snowstorm hit and Bart was at a friend's house, and you and the olders and your ex-wife got stranded at the Bar all night? That was the year my marriage had started falling apart. Mitzi and I were here at the inn, alone, and it was late, and we started talking…" George trails off and gestures for the flask, and Kelley hands it to him. "You know how things like that sometimes happen, Kelley. Come on. That was the year you turned fifty. You were miserable, and so was Mitzi. You were at the Bar all night with your ex-wife, for God's sake."

"Wait," Kelley says. "Wait a minute." He vaguely remembers the year George is talking about, but it's like an episode of a sitcom that has gone off the air.

The year he turned fifty…it was a bad year; he remembers that much. Bart would have been seven, in second grade, Mrs. Usbiff—the year Bart nearly got held back; she put his desk out in the hallway. Ava was seventeen, a senior in high school; she didn't get in to Juilliard or Curtis. That had been a disaster, and Margaret blamed Kelley because he was the one who had taken Ava out of New York City and away from her piano teacher, Mr. Masahiro. Ava could have stayed in the city with Margaret, but she would have been dropped off and picked up from piano lessons by Raoul and fed her meals by Lotus. Kelley hadn't thought that was any way to raise a child.

Kevin had dropped out of the Culinary Institute that year as well, thanks to the nefarious Norah Vale. And the inn had a bad leak that precipitated the replacement of the entire roof, to the tune of forty-five grand.

It had not been a good year. Kelley and Mitzi engaged in low-level ground fire, a baseline of incessant bickering and sarcasm. He remembers a string of three nights when Mitzi had stayed with her friend Kai the Massage Therapist out in Pocomo. Mitzi had been angry that Margaret was coming to visit for the holidays, but Margaret had insisted because it was Ava's last year of high school and she wanted to be with her kids—and because of the traditions Kelley and Mitzi had started, the kids wanted to be at the inn.

The three older kids had been excited to see Margaret. All of the Quinns, including Mitzi, had gone for dinner at the Brotherhood, where it had started really snowing, which everyone loved because it was two days before Christmas. Kevin had encouraged them all to go to the Bar for a nightcap, and everyone was game except for Mitzi. Mitzi had dropped Bart off at his friend Michael's house, and then she went home. George had probably been sitting by the fire, drinking a tumbler of Johnnie Walker Black, and Mitzi—feeling left out, abandoned, and angry—would naturally have joined him.

"Are you suggesting that if I hadn't gone to the Bar that night ... ?" Kelley says.

"With Margaret and your older kids," George says. He

shifts his weight, and Kelley realizes it's rude to continue to make the man stand, so he scoots over and pats the edge of the bed, indicating that George should sit. George looks relieved to take a load off. "Well, you know, Mitzi has always been threatened by Margaret."

"Who hasn't?" Kelley says. "She's Margaret Quinn."

"I mean, by your relationship with Margaret," George says. "And, to some extent, by your relationship with the olders. I think she felt they were your 'real' family, and she and Bart were…latecomers to the party."

"Oh," Kelley says. He has heard Mitzi articulate a version of this argument in the past, but he always dismissed her words as insecure and ridiculous. He had been married to Mitzi for twenty-one years, and he was married to Margaret for only nineteen. Still, Margaret came first. She is, by Kelley's own nomenclature, the original Margaret, and they had three kids and a really cool brownstone and an enviable life in Manhattan before they self-destructed. Kelley and Margaret grew into adults and then professionals and then parents together. There was a way in which Margaret wasn't replaceable, although Kelley had never expressed this sentiment, even to himself, and certainly never to Mitzi.

"I gave Mitzi everything she wanted," Kelley says. "I quit my job for her, I left New York for her, I moved to Nantucket for her. I bought this inn—this inn specifically, because she had stayed here—and I restored it to her exact specifications, George, which, by the way, nearly bankrupted me."

George nods sympathetically, as if he is well acquainted with seeing his personal fortune slowly go down the drain. Kelley realizes he doesn't know what George does for a living. Is that *possible* after so many years? But the only occupation Kelley can come up with for George is professional Santa Claus. Surely that's not all he does?

"What's your line of work, George?" Kelley asks. "If you've told me before, I've forgotten."

"I'm a milliner," George says. "I make hats. Fine hats, for women. I have a shop in Lenox, and a website, which has tripled my business. Two years ago, Oprah picked my straw boater as one of her Favorite Things, and even now, demand far exceeds supply. My problem, quite honestly, is that I'd like to work less rather than more, but I don't see that happening for quite a while."

"You're a *milliner*," Kelley says. He finds this funny and quaint. He would have predicted that George was a salesman for a drug company or a liquor distributor.

"I learned from my father, who learned from his father," George says. "But the skill set dies with me, since I never had children."

Now that George is with Mitzi, he will have some kind of relationship with Bart as well. Kelley tries to imagine Bart learning the skill set of a milliner, and the mere thought puts a smile on Kelley's face for the first time since he opened the door to room 10 the day before.

"I've never known Mitzi to wear hats," Kelley says.

"She hates hats," George says.

They sit with that statement in silence. Kelley takes a drink from the flask. George dabs his bloodied handkerchief at his swollen lip. Just outside the door, Kelley can hear the strains of "Angels We Have Heard on High." Ava must have altered the inn's playlist since Mitzi's departure. Mitzi prefers nonreligious carols; she is a big fan of "Silver Bells" and Andy Williams singing "Sleigh Ride." But Ava thinks religious carols have more musical integrity. Now that Mitzi is gone, she can have her way.

Glooooooooooooooria!

"Thank you for seeing me," George says. "I feel better."

"I don't," Kelley says. This is a lie. He does feel better, but he isn't quite ready for the conversation to be over. "Do you think Mitzi leaving me has anything to do with Bart?"

"Of course," George says. "Her son has flown from the nest. It calls all kinds of other things into question, such as, how much does she like the nest? And, what is she doing in the nest? And, you know, she didn't want him to go. She saw in her crystals that harm would come to him. Surely she told you that?"

"She told me that," Kelley says. "Surely *you* don't believe in...*crystals?*"

"No," George says. "Not really."

Kelley takes "not really" to mean "not at all." He says, "You weren't born on February twenty-ninth, too, were you?"

"June first," George says. He clears his throat. "The point

is, Kelley, that *Mitzi* believes in the crystals. She felt like you made Bart go to war anyway."

"Bart wanted to go," Kelley says.

"Mitzi feels like you forced the issue."

"Untrue," Kelley says. On this, he will stand firm. He did have a come-to-Jesus with Bart after his last run-in with the Nantucket Police. Kelley told his son that he had to do something, go somewhere, try to make something of his life. He could go to Colorado and ski, he could work his way through Europe bartending, he could go to Cape Cod Community College. But he could not stay on Nantucket and sponge off Kelley and Mitzi and continue to get in trouble with the law and desecrate the family name. Bart came up with the Marines himself.

George shrugs like it's not his place to get involved, and he's right about that.

"What are you and Mitzi going to *do?*" Kelley asks. "Are you going to open an inn in Lenox?"

George laughs, then winces in pain. "No way. I'd rather eat glass. And Mitzi is all done with innkeeping. She's been sick of it for a while."

"She *has?*" Kelley says. This is news to him. Mitzi has been as gung ho about the inn this year as ever, and as disconsolate about the steady decline in guests. Because Kelley and Mitzi became so involved in their guests' lives — they once visited the Pipers at their home in Long Beach, California, and they've been invited to countless weddings of the guests that became engaged at the inn—it's hard not to take the vacancies as a personal affront.

"She wants to get trained and certified as a life coach," George says.

Kelley barks out laughter. A *life coach?* That's even funnier than picturing Bart as a milliner! Mitzi *needs* a life coach! She needs someone to set her straight: running off with George the Santa Claus is a terrible mistake. She should sit tight and stay with Kelley. They can sell the inn; they are going to *have* to sell the inn if they want to survive financially, and then they can figure out a next step.

The thought of Mitzi becoming trained and certified as a life coach is absurd. She might say that Kelley is belittling her hopes and dreams; she might say he doesn't believe in her now and, furthermore, never has. Kelley would point to the four-thousand-dollar claw-foot bathtub as antique-porcelain proof that he has believed in her and pursued her every desire all these years.

But, Kelley thinks.

But wouldn't Mitzi be right, in a way?

Isn't it true that he never took Mitzi's career aspirations, her intellect, her *personhood,* as seriously as he took Margaret's?

Admit it. Yes.

It's true. A part of him always thought Mitzi lacked gravitas. *Mitzi is ditzy.* In the most private, hidden corridors of his mind, Kelley might have thought Mitzi a bit silly. It's the gold-lamé-jumpsuit-and-disco-ball persona that transmogrified into her crystal-reading-and-herbal-tea-blends-innkeeper persona that he indulges rather than reveres. He indulges her because, decades earlier, when he started dating Mitzi, his primary emotion was gratitude that Mitzi wanted him, Kelley Quinn, and not an exclusive interview with Yasser Arafat.

"Did Mitzi ever tell you how she and I met?" Kelley asks George. "It's an interesting story."

"I'd like to hear it," George says, and Kelley thinks, *Wow, George is a pretty evolved man if he doesn't mind listening to this.*

"Are you sure you have time?" Kelley says. "I'm not keeping you from anything?" He wants to ask George where Mitzi is... but he figures that will kill his mood and the conversation, regardless of the answer.

"Not at all," George says. "Fire away."

And so, Kelley tells the story of how he first saw Mitzi in Greenwich Village, standing outside the brownstone of Kelley's brother, Avery, who was dying of AIDS.

"I noticed Mitzi because she was beautiful," Kelley says.

"Stunning, I'm sure," George says.

"But I talked to her because she was wearing a T-shirt from the Straight Wharf on Nantucket. You know the Straight Wharf logo, the bluefish?"

"I do, indeed," George says.

Kelley had asked Mitzi about her connection to Nantucket.

He was interested, he said, because he and his ex-wife had taken their kids to the island for a string of summers, and he really loved it.

Mitzi told Kelley that she had been to Nantucket once for a wedding, and now she went for a week every summer and stayed at the Winter Street Inn.

Kelley said he knew of the Winter Street Inn. He had passed it many times on his amblings through town.

They shared their Nantucket favorites — Kelley's favorite beach was Cisco; Mitzi's, Steps; Kelley's favorite bar, 21 Federal; Mitzi's, the Gazebo.

"The Gazebo?" Kelley said. "That's a bar for kids in their twenties."

Mitzi had smiled at Kelley, and he realized that Mitzi was in her twenties, which meant she was ten or fifteen years younger than he. Which meant he had a choice: he could walk away, or he could ask Mitzi out and become a clichéd divorced guy on the brink of forty asking out a twenty-something-year-old.

He walked away. His brother was expecting him upstairs, anyway.

"But then," Kelley says, "a miraculous thing happened."

"You bumped into her again?" George guesses.

"Yes," Kelley says. "At the moment I least expected."

Avery, Kelley's brother, died of pneumonia in September of 1992. Mitzi showed up at Avery's funeral.

"You're kidding," George says.

"I wouldn't kid about something like that," Kelley says.

"Of course not," George says. "I'm sorry for the loss of your brother."

"He was a fine, fine human being," Kelley says. "One of the finest." He takes a deep breath, remembering the funeral at Grace Church. The sanctuary had been packed with men—young and old, healthy and sick. It was the early nineties in Greenwich Village; everyone was going through the same thing.

Margaret hadn't been able to attend the funeral because it was only two months before the election, and she was on the road, following the Clinton campaign.

Kelley remembers seeing Mitzi sitting in the second pew, wearing peach instead of black, which was a welcome respite for the eyes. He knew he'd seen her before, but he couldn't place where.

"It was she who approached me at the reception," Kelley says. "She came up to me and said, 'I met you outside the brownstone. We talked about Nantucket. You like Cisco Beach. I'm Mitzi Kelleher.'"

"Wow," George says. "Lucky you!"

"Turned out she was a childhood friend of Avery's partner, Marcus. And when I saw her the first time, she had just come from their apartment. She had taken the train up from Philadelphia to lend Marcus moral support."

"Unbelievable," George says.

"She was only twenty-four, though," Kelley says. "But by

that point, standing in my brother's funeral reception when my brother had been only thirty-six himself, I realized life is too short to worry about being thought a cliché. So I asked her out."

"Good man," George says.

Kelley takes a minute to reflect on just how profoundly meeting Mitzi had changed his life. She had saved him from his misery and his self-destructive ways. It had been nothing short of amazing.

But over the years, of course, Kelley's feelings of ecstasy settled and matured in correspondence with life's circumstances. He and Mitzi got married and had a child. They bought the inn and started the business of running it. Meanwhile, in New York, Margaret grew more and more famous, and Kelley's respect for her career increased. There she was, in 2000, standing in front of the Florida State House. There she was, interviewing Al Gore! But it was 9/11 that really changed things. Margaret was new to CBS, working as a "special correspondent," which meant they were throwing her into every possible situation, night and day, and seeing how she fared. On that particular Tuesday, they were short staffed, and Margaret lived only a few blocks from the studio in Midtown and could be there in minutes. Kelley can still remember turning on the TV to see *what was happening*—because who, initially, understood?—and there, on his screen, was Margaret. She was at the epicenter of one of the most important news stories the world would ever know. The north tower tumbled to the ground behind her like something in a big-budget action movie, and Margaret turned around, incredulous; you could see it in her eyes. She started to weep. *So many American lives have been lost,* she said. *Wow,* she said. *Oh my God, oh my God, oh my God.* Kelley wanted to reach into his television set and hold her, comfort her. Margaret Quinn was strong, but she wasn't invincible. Their city, the city where they had raised a family and made a mess of everything, was under attack. Kelley had confided these feelings to Mitzi later that night. *I wanted to offer Margaret some comfort. I tried to call her but couldn't get through.* Mitzi had stiffened in his embrace. Maybe she had thought, *He still loves her.* Maybe she had thought, *What about me? What about our son?*

Kelley is wise enough to realize that his marriage to Mitzi isn't ending *because of George.* That is facile thinking. There have been fault lines ever since 9/11.

And then, the following year, when Kelley turned fifty, he agreed to let Margaret come for Christmas, and a snowstorm hit, and Kelley and Margaret ended up stuck at the Bar with the olders. The roads had been impassable, and it became clear they would be stuck at the Bar for the night. Kevin fetched pillows and blankets from the band house, and Margaret and Ava curled up on the pool tables while Kelley and Patrick and Kevin drank the night away, listening to vintage Led Zeppelin.

Kelley remembers the contentedness of that night, a

feeling, as he looked at the reclining figure of Margaret, that something had been set right and the mistakes they'd made when the kids were young had been corrected—or, if not corrected, then forgiven.

He hadn't missed Mitzi or wished she was there. He doesn't remember thinking about Mitzi at all.

And now this.

Kelley takes a slug from George's monogrammed flask. In the rest of the house, he hears...footsteps, voices, a new carol playing on the inn's sound system. "Silent Night," his all-time favorite. Ava and Kevin and Isabelle will be getting ready for the party. Kelley had expected to sit out the party in the dark, quiet, acrid-smelling cocoon of his bedroom, but now he finds he wants to be among people who believe in him. This is *his* family tradition: the Christmas Eve party at the Winter Street Inn.

AVA

Christmas on Nantucket, Ava has learned, is like summertime on Nantucket in miniature. There is an enormous amount of build-up and preparation (*Get ready! Get ready!*), then it happens (*Enjoy every second!*), then it's over (*Too quickly!*). And once it's over, a certain melancholy encroaches. What is the saddest day of the year—Labor Day or December 26?

With this in mind, Ava tells herself to *be present* and *celebrate* the holiday instead of wishing it over. After all, one is given only a certain number of Christmases in one's life.

At ten minutes to seven, she checks her cell phone: no messages from Nathaniel. She isn't surprised by this—he said he would call after the Cabots' party—but some unpleasant scenarios take up space in Ava's mind. She imagines the Cabots' house as large and gracious and impeccably decorated with family heirlooms and greens cut from their rolling acreage. She imagines bottles of vintage Dom Pérignon being popped and vodka tumbling over ice. Someone will place the order at Pizza Post for half a dozen cheesesteaks and two large pies with everything, plus extra olives, which is exactly what they've ordered for the past twenty-five years. Kirsten's parents, the elder Cabots, would treat Nathaniel like part of the family. He'd gone to school with Kirsten since kindergarten at Greenwich Country Day, and they'd started dating sophomore year, while they were both at St. George's, so there were a lot of memories, a lot of stories. Mr. Cabot might invite Nathaniel into his study for a Cuban cigar, where Mr. Cabot would confide that he's glad Kirsten is done with that Bimal fellow; Bimal never really fit in. Mr. Cabot won't say outright that it's because Bimal isn't white, but really, what else could he mean?

That scenario is bad, but it's preferable to Nathaniel and Kirsten deciding to ditch the older adults and grabbing a bottle of the vintage Dom to drink up in Kirsten's bedroom. Or Nathaniel and Kirsten being dispatched to pick up the pizza and cheesesteaks and, possibly, getting lost accidentally on purpose on the way.

Stop it! Ava tells herself. Her imagination is her own worst enemy. The tequila shot did her no favors.

Maybe Nathaniel is trapped on the Cabots' dog-hair-covered sofa between his mother and Mrs. Cabot, wishing he were flying with Ava to Hawaii. Maybe when Kirsten asks him if he wants to steal a bottle of Dom from the ice bucket and go up to her room, he will remember that she is a little bit psycho. Maybe he will remember the summer between his junior and senior years in high school, when he road-tripped to a Phish concert in Albany with his best friend, Alex, and Kirsten was so jealous that she called him saying she had viral meningitis and was being admitted to Fairfield Hospital. Nathaniel turned the car around and missed the Phish concert, only to find Kirsten at home on the sofa, with a wet washcloth over her eyes. Not meningitis, just a garden-variety headache, self-inflicted.

At five minutes to seven, the doorbell rings. Mrs. Gabler, on cue. Ava tucks her phone under her pillow and promises herself she won't check it again until the party is over and she's finished cleaning up. If she misses Nathaniel's call, she misses his call. She will remedy her lie by telling him that she decided not to go to Hawaii after all—because she is badly needed here.

She *is* badly needed here.

It's showtime.

With everything that's happened, Ava expects the party to be a disaster—but it's as much fun as ever, if not more. Would it be awful for Ava to say that's because Mitzi and George aren't attending? Is it possible that their absence, instead of ruining the party, has made it better? Because Mitzi is gone, Ava is the hostess. The black velvet dress looks even nicer on her tonight than it did in the dressing room at Hepburn. Ava's skin glows pearlescent, and her dark-red hair and green eyes pop. She probably looks this good once every five years. When Scott sees her in the dress, his eyes get very big and round, and he lets a whistle escape. Ava twirls. She feels pretty, she feels sexy—and stupid, stinky Nathaniel is missing it!

Scott says, "Ava, you look enchanting." He's speaking in a British accent; "enchanting" is *"enchohnting."* The British accent is probably also the result of the tequila, but people love it. Mrs. Gabler takes one look at Scott and says, "Oh, thank heavens, a younger Santa!" Scott then tells Mrs. Gabler how captivating she looks. His accent is thick and plummy, perfectly executed, and Ava sees Scott in a slightly different light. He has a new energy, he's dynamic and charming and extroverted and very un-Scott-like. He calls himself Father Christmas, delighting the children and the ladies. Kevin is plying Scott with tequila shots, which he does discreetly in the alcove under the stairs, but Ava has seen Scott drunk many times before, and she knows his new confidence isn't solely due to the alcohol.

Isabelle looks *adorable* in Mitzi's Mrs. Claus dress! Her hair is in long braids, the way Ava likes it best, and she's wearing black-satin kitten heels instead of the dominatrix boots that Mitzi favored. She looks like a character plucked right from Tolstoy, a Russian princess.

Ava pulls Isabelle over to meet Scott. "Mrs. Claus," she says, "meet your Mr. Claus, otherwise known as Scott Skyler."

"Oh!" Isabelle says. *"Bon soir!"* She curtseys and offers Scott her hand.

"Santa, Isabelle will be playing the part of your lovely wife tonight. Isabelle works with us here at the inn."

"Charmed," Scott says in his British accent. He kisses Isabelle's hand.

Excellent! Ava thinks. Scott and Isabelle gaze at each other for an extended moment, or so it seems to Ava. Her plan is working.

Then—surprise! surprise!—a cheer goes up in the room. Kelley has made an appearance! He's wearing his red-and-green wool tartan trousers, just as he does every year, and he's holding aloft a magnum of Perrier-Jouët. He moves through the crowd to place the magnum in the large brass ice bucket near the front door. Later, he will saber the top off into the front yard, a feat he only performs on even-numbered years.

Ava thought her father might have abandoned the champagne-sabering tradition, given the circumstances, but Kelley looks proud and happy; he transports the champagne like he's carrying a baby. Then he takes Ava by the arm. "You look beautiful, sweetheart. You remind me so much of your mother."

Ava's heart swells. The ultimate compliment. "Thank you, Daddy. What happened to George?"

"He left out the back door," Kelley says. "But I think he wanted to stay."

"I'm sure he did," Ava says. She knows that somewhere on this island, Mitzi is wishing she were here. The party is in full swing: the room is crowded with familiar faces, there is talking and laughing, Kevin is flipping bottles and mixing his drinks from great height. He stops to juggle lemons and limes, and people applaud. Kevin is the King of Fascinating Bar Tricks. Scott takes his seat in the wingback armchair, with Isabelle at his side. She lines up the children—almost all of them students at the elementary school. If they know Father Christmas is Assistant Principal Skyler, no one lets on.

Ava grabs a glass of white wine from Kevin at the bar. "What do you think about Isabelle in Mitzi's dress?" she asks.

"I was never a particular fan of that dress," he says. "But she looks fine, I guess."

"I'm trying to set her up with Scott," Ava says.

Kevin, who is as nimble a bartender as one will ever meet, nearly drops a highball glass and the bottle of Jack Daniel's he's holding. *"What?"* he says.

"I think they'd be cute together, don't you?"

"No," Kevin says, with what sounds like genuine anger. "I do not think they would be cute together. What is *wrong* with you, Ava?"

Ava is speechless. Kevin never gets angry with her. Kevin is her prime ally in this family. Ava wanders away, wondering if he's right to be mad. Maybe it *is* terribly manipulative to try to fix up Scott with someone else just because she doesn't want him.

Well, her intentions were pure. She won't let Kevin ruin her good mood or her fun time.

Ava has a few minutes yet before she has to sit down at the piano and start the carols. She hits the food table; she's been so busy getting ready for the party that she hasn't had anything to eat all day. She fixes herself a plate of cocktail ribs and Swedish meatballs, which are disappearing fast—there is beef at the Winter Street Inn Christmas Eve party for the first time ever! On top of everything else, Isabelle is a phenomenal cook! Ava must mention this to Scott—who cares what Kevin says! She takes two dates stuffed with peanut butter and some scallop seviche and a mini crab cake. She even drags a cracker through the salted-almond pinecone and eats it right away. Delicious!

She makes a plate for Scott and then a plate for Kevin, as a peace offering—both heavy on the meatballs—adding deviled eggs, spanakopita triangles, and cherry tomatoes stuffed with guacamole. It's nice to be able to load up her own plate. When Mitzi was in charge, there was strict adherence to Family Hold Back. Mitzi was always worried they were going to run out of food; she once took a celery stick out of Ava's hand and set it back down on the crudité platter.

This party does not miss Mitzi. Ava does not miss Mitzi.

Fun, fun, fun, chitchat, happy holidays! Everyone who is anyone is there, and people keep streaming through the door—all five Nantucket selectmen; the police chief, Ed Kapenash, and his wife, Andrea; Gene Mahon, aka "Mahon about Town"; Jordan Randolph, the editor of the paper, and his son, Jake, who is a junior at Penn; the real-estate agent Eddie Pancik and his wife, Grace; and many of Ava's fellow teachers from school, including her friend Shelby. Shelby grabs Ava by the arm and says, "Is that *Scott* in the Santa suit? Because he looks *good.* He looks, I don't know, kinda *hot,* don't you think?"

"Well...?" Ava says. Shelby is of the opinion that Ava should break up with Nathaniel and date Scott. Nathaniel is too much work; Shelby is sick of watching Ava try to persuade Nathaniel to love her. Whereas Scott already loves her. "He's doing a British-accent thingy."

"British accent?" Shelby says. "Scott?" She nudges Ava. "That's hot, too, right? It's very *Downton Abbey.*"

"It's weird," Ava says. "It's like he's someone else."

"And who's the chick?" Shelby asks.

"Isabelle," Ava says. "She works for us. She's French."

"She's stunning."

Ava decides not to tell Shelby that she's trying to set Scott and Isabelle up; Shelby might not like the idea any better than Kevin did.

Ava and Shelby find themselves moving close enough to Scott that they can eavesdrop. He has Micah Daniels, the terror of the entire kindergarten class, up on his lap, but for once Micah is quiet, awestruck. It's Father Christmas.

"Hello, young chap," Scott says. "What is your name?"

"Micah Daniels."

"Micah Daniels! Capital, capital! And tell me, Micah Daniels, have you been a good boy this year? Have you been polite and respectful to your parents and…your teachers?"

Micah nods solemnly, and Ava rolls her eyes. This is the kid who brought a Chinese star to school and stuck it in another student's hot dog. This is the kid who called his teacher, Mrs. Peale, an "old fat ass."

"Are you *sure* about that, Micah Daniels? Because, you know, Father Christmas watches you night and day, at school and at home. I check in with your parents, and also with… Mrs. Peale."

Micah looks sufficiently intimidated. Ava is waiting for Scott to say that Micah is getting COAL, NOTHING BUT COAL—or at the very least that he is lingering on some sort of Undecided List, a Santa Claus Limbo. But Scott has mercy.

"And what, Micah Daniels, is your heart's greatest desire for Christmas morning?"

Shelby mouths, *Xbox.*

Micah says, "Xbox."

Isabelle steps back a few feet to take the picture with the Winter Street Inn digital camera—photos later to be posted on Facebook—but before she snaps it, Scott says, "Ho-ho-ho, Mrs. Claus, why don't you get in the picture?"

Isabelle lowers the camera. *"Excusez-moi?"*

Scott waves her in. "Come, be in the picture. Ava will take it, won't you, Ava?"

Ava hands her glass of wine off to Shelby. "Certainly, yes, of course." She accepts the camera from Isabelle, thinking she can't blame Scott for not wanting his picture taken alone with the nightmare that is Micah Daniels. Isabelle will improve it. *A spoonful of sugar helps the medicine go down...*

Isabelle stands next to Scott and slides her arm around his superhero shoulders and tilts her pretty blond head so that it practically rests against Scott's. When Ava looks through the viewfinder, she is shocked to find that she is bothered by their pose. She is...jealous. Scott, Isabelle, and Micah Daniels look like a family, which of course they're *not,* although if Scott and Isabelle *do* start dating and get married, they may find themselves in a similar pose in the not-too-distant future.

Ava does not like it.

Wow.

She's confused.

She grits her teeth and beams at Scott, Isabelle, and Micah. "Smile!" she says. She takes the picture, and the flash goes off.

Scott says, "Take another one!"

She takes another one.

Ava has to go to the ladies' room, so she heads to the back of the inn. She doesn't know what just happened with Scott. She thinks of Kevin saying, *What is* wrong *with you, Ava?* There isn't anything wrong with her. She is setting Scott and Isabelle up so that the two of them can find happiness together. Maybe she's bothered because Scott has always been hers and hers alone. But Ava doesn't want Scott, right? She wants the mind, body, and soul of Nathaniel Oscar, maker of fancy and special pantry doors.

The party is fun, and she has a nice glow, although she is far from drunk, which is good, because she still has to play the carols.

She will not check her phone. It's ten after eight. She will not check her phone.

She checks her phone.

Nothing from Nathaniel. Her heart breaks a little.

There are two texts: one from Patrick and one from her mother.

Patrick: *asdhaosihdkqebrkb.* (Butt dial? Or incredibly drunk? Ava doesn't care.)

Margaret: *Oh, honey...* (Margaret forgot what she was going to say? She got interrupted? Or "Oh, honey" is a general statement of guilt because she can't take Ava to Hawaii? Ava doesn't care.)

She sits on the edge of her bed and takes a deep breath. Oxygen.

Why did she check her phone?

She goes back to the party.

MARGARET

She wears a red dress that clashes with her hair; imploring Roger again for the silver Audrey Hepburn did no good. It's Christmas Eve; it has to be red. The broadcast is light, so light that it primarily consists of footage of Christmas Eve celebrations from around the world—fireworks over the Eiffel Tower in Paris, Pope Francis I saying Mass in St. Peter's Square.

Margaret smiles into the camera. Her favorite cameraman, Ernest, is five foot three, and he's wearing an elf hat and a necklace of glowing chili pepper lights.

"For CBS News, I'm Margaret Quinn, wishing all of you a safe and happy holiday and peace for the coming year." Margaret holds...she holds...This is by far her least favorite part of the job, smiling into the vacant eye of the camera for all of America when she's done and ready to move on.

"And...cut!" her producer, Mickey Benz, says. "Good job, Margaret. Enjoy Hawaii."

Merry Christmas, Margaret, enjoy Hawaii, have fun, you deserve it. She does deserve it! She spends only twelve week-days a year out of people's living rooms — five days in August, Thanksgiving Day and the Friday after, and five days at Christmas. Cynthia, the office manager, has left a bottle of SPF 75 sunblock next to Margaret's computer with a note that says, *Protect the most famous face in America.* Margaret smiles and throws the sunscreen in her bag. She extends the handle of her suitcase and checks her phone. She has a single text. It's from Drake. He's already at Newark, in Terminal C, waiting for her at the outpost of Grand Central Oyster Bar with a dozen Malpeques ordered.

Are you close?

Margaret chuckles. This is exactly what he asks her when they're making love.

On my way! she texts back. She's relieved there are no texts from Nantucket. She assumes everyone is carrying on with his or her Christmas Eve festivities. She'll call tomorrow.

Then Margaret looks up, and, like a Ferrari smashing into a brick wall, she sees Darcy's face right up in hers, and Darcy is not happy.

"Margaret," she says.

Margaret's heart does a free fall.

"What?" Margaret says. She thinks, *I am two hundred yards from the exit of the building, where Raoul is waiting for me with the car. I have a dozen Malpeques, a glass of champagne, and a very cute surgeon anticipating my imminent arrival. And then Hawaii, Darcy, a suite at the Four Seasons, a level of luxury you have not yet known in your young life. I deserve this vacation—everyone just said so. Please, don't tell me that Michelle Obama has filed for divorce, don't tell me aliens have landed on Soldier Field. I don't want to know. I don't care.*

Darcy holds out a piece of paper that looks suspiciously like a briefing sheet.

Margaret shakes her head.

"Read it," Darcy whispers.

A convoy carrying forty-five American troops headed out of Sangin, Afghanistan, was intercepted by insurgent forces. The troops are thought to be alive. *They were marched off rather than shot on sight,* Margaret thinks. They will be held, treated abominably, possibly tortured, and used as bargaining chips.

Margaret looks at Darcy. "You don't have names, do you?"

Darcy shakes her head. No names, nothing definite, and yet somehow Margaret knows why Darcy brought this to her. Bart Quinn is among the forty-five; Margaret feels it in her gut.

She calls Drake to cancel.

AVA

"Deck the Halls."

"Frosty the Snowman."

"Up on the Housetop."

"Rudolph."

"Silver Bells."

"Winter Wonderland."

"Chestnuts Roasting."

"Sleigh Ride."

"The Little Drummer Boy"—this is Ava's insertion. It would be too religious for Mitzi, but Mitzi isn't here!

She says to Kelley, "I'll take one more." She bows her head and squeezes her eyes shut. Her hands are inadvertently arched over the C chord, which is how "Jingle Bells" starts— although her heart's greatest desire this Christmas is that tonight will end without her having to play it.

"Jingle Bells," someone/everyone yells.

Ava plays "Jingle Bells" and even gives it a little extra gusto as she suddenly remembers Claire Frye and her father, Gavin, and Ava's vow to play the song in Claire's honor. Besides, she won't have to play it again for 364 days. Then she segues into "We Wish You a Merry Christmas," signaling the end of the caroling. Her father and Scott are at the piano, arms wrapped around each other.

As soon as the last chord evaporates into the pine-scented air, there is the sound of a spoon chiming against a glass. Ava looks up. This is unusual. Normally now is when people start to file out.

Kevin is standing on top of the Igloo boat cooler. He looks like he has an announcement to make; he is probably trying to take over the reins from their father and thank everyone for coming. This will hasten the exodus even more.

When the room quiets down, Kevin hands the glass and the spoon off to a bystander and says, "Isabelle Beaulieu? Mrs. Claus? Isabelle, where are you?"

Huh? Ava thinks.

Isabelle is now circulating with a tray of hors d'oeuvres, but she turns and gazes up at Kevin.

Kevin pulls a velvet box out of his pocket and says, "Isabelle Beaulieu, will you marry me?"

Kevin and Isabelle—*together? As in, lovers? Kevin is proposing?*

Then a second thought hits her sideways: Isabelle *is* pregnant, and *THE BABY IS KEVIN'S!*

People are shocked, stunned, stupefied! No one more so than Ava. But everyone loves an unexpected proposal, especially at Christmas. The room roars!

Ava sways. Scott materializes at her side. She looks up at him in his Father Christmas hat. She doesn't know which emotion overwhelms her more—surprise happiness for

Kevin and Isabelle, or surprise relief that Scott will not be dating Isabelle. She thinks of Kevin's reaction when she told him she was setting up Scott and Isabelle—*that* was why he was so angry.

Together, she and Scott watch as Isabelle—it seems belatedly understanding what is happening—approaches Kevin. She is holding both hands over her mouth, she is trembling and crying—with joy, it seems, unadulterated joy. Watching her, Ava tears up herself. Isabelle and Kevin are in love! She can't believe it!

She involuntarily compares the expression of Isabelle's face now—she looks like someone who just won ten million dollars and a dream house in Tahiti—with the expression Norah Vale wore when *she* was in Kevin's presence. Which, even on her wedding day, could be most accurately described as somewhere between dour and snarling.

Ava is so happy for Kevin. He deserves this. Even though Ava had hoped to be the one getting engaged tonight, she feels nothing but elation at the turn of events.

Kevin slips the ring on Isabelle's finger, and the crowd cheers. Scott lets a wolf whistle fly, loud enough to summon every dog in the neighborhood.

Kevin jumps down to kiss Isabelle, and Ava's father moves for the magnum of champagne. It's clearly time for the sabering, and now they really have something to celebrate! Kelley pulls his saber out of the umbrella stand, opens the front door, and holds the bottom of the champagne bottle against his belt buckle. In one fluid motion, he slices the top of the bottle off; it flies into the yard. This is a trick he learned one year when he went to Paris with Margaret, supposedly taught to him by the personal sommelier of François Mitterrand. It dazzles every time.

As Kelley pours glasses of the Perrier-Jouët, Ava wonders: Did her father *know* Kevin and Isabelle were together? Did he know this proposal was in the works? Does he know Isabelle is pregnant?

Scott accepts two flutes of champagne and hands one to Ava. They clink glasses.

"Cheers!" she says. "I can't believe it."

"You were trying to set me up with Isabelle," Scott says, "weren't you?"

"Oh, hush," Ava says. "The two of you would have made a cute couple, too."

"You were jealous," Scott says. "I saw it on your face."

"Was not."

"Yes, you were. When you took the picture of me, Isabelle, and the Holy Terror, you looked angry. Jealous angry."

Ava barely suppresses a smile. She drinks her champagne. "Shut up."

"Admit it."

"I will not admit it," she says. "But I will give you this."

"What?"

"You make one hell of a Santa."

KEVIN

I love you," Isabelle says.

"And I love you," Kevin says. He holds Isabelle's left hand and kisses her finger. He bought her the best ring in the store, from a girl he went to high school with named Phoebe Showalter.

Phoebe asked him who the ring was for and he said, "I can't tell you that yet."

Isabelle is trembling—whether because of the pregnancy or her delirious happiness, he can't say.

He almost didn't summon the courage to buy the ring. He kept thinking of Norah Vale, and how much he'd loved her, how much he had invested in her, and all the ways he'd changed the course of his life to please her. First, he left Ann Arbor, even though he'd been happy there. He liked the other students, liked his professors, enjoyed the school spirit at the football games; he'd also gotten the best grades of his life. But Norah was miserable. She didn't look for a job, didn't make friends, and didn't like the friends that Kevin made.

Poughkeepsie and the CIA were better. A lot of his classmates were tattooed and pierced and did drugs or drank too much, and Norah felt more comfortable among them. It wasn't so "rah-rah," she said. She got a job waitressing, at the Palace Diner, but then, in Kevin's final year, she got fired for cursing out a family of six who had only left her a ten-cent tip. She screamed profanities at them in the diner's parking lot and was canned pretty much on the spot.

So it was back to Nantucket for the two of them, where Kelley lent Kevin and Norah enough money to put a down payment on a house. They limped along for a few more years, until Norah started hanging out with a guy named Jonas who drove a taxi and sold heroin, and Kevin had no self-respecting option but to ask her for a divorce. They sold the house; Norah took the money and left.

No more women, Kevin vowed.

He kept making excuses *not* to enter the jewelry store. He needed a coffee, and then he needed a sandwich from the pharmacy lunch counter. Town started filling with people, and he saw Gibby the inn's summer landscaper first, then Cheesy, whom he'd gone to high school with, and he stopped to talk. Cheesy had his five-year-old with him, and the kid was jumping up and down, shouting about how Santa was coming and he had made a list, and he was going to leave milk and cookies, and carrots for the reindeer, and glitter in the yard so the reindeer could find his house, and Kevin thought, *I am going to have a child; I had better get my ass into the jewelry store.* Main Street was buzzing with happy, excited energy. The trees were lit up, and the shops had their doors wide-open for last-minute shoppers; most were serving cookies and cider. The Victorian carolers were strolling in their elaborate period costumes, like something right out of Mitzi's display at home. As the carolers passed Kevin, he heard them singing "Good King Wenceslas." Was it going to snow? It was still too warm, but maybe, *maybe* tomorrow...

Kevin lollygagged for so long that it became time for the red-ticket drawing, run by the Chamber of Commerce. If you bought anything from a Chamber member during the month of December, you received red tickets. Now that it was three o'clock, the tickets were being pulled by the town crier. There would be five one-thousand-dollar winners and one five-thousand-dollar winner.

Kevin found a strip of seven red tickets in his wallet. He thought about how great it would be if he won.

The five one-thousand-dollar winners were picked. Not his number, not even close. He nearly left because he knew Ava would be on the verge of a nervous breakdown, wondering where he was.

But then, the big moment! The five-thousand-dollar winner was...!

I will pay my mother back, Kevin thought. *Or I will put the money right into an account for the baby.*

But the number called wasn't Kevin's. The winning red ticket belonged to Eric Metz, who was a mechanic at Don Allen Ford and the father of six kids, one of whom was severely autistic. The crowd roared! It was always best when a local person won, not to mention a person so deserving. Five thousand dollars would mean a lot to the Metz family, especially at Christmas. But when Eric Metz went up to turn in his winning ticket, he announced that he was donating the entire five thousand dollars to Nantucket Hospice, which had taken such excellent care of his mother when she was dying of lymphoma.

The crowd was silent for a second—perhaps acknowledging that they might not be so generous with a sudden windfall—then there was an even louder roar of applause, whistles, and calls of approval.

Kevin experienced an unfamiliar feeling. He knew he had just witnessed an act of grace, and all he could think was that he wanted to emulate Eric Metz going forward.

He had walked right into the jewelry store and told Phoebe Showalter he needed a diamond ring.

And now, he and Isabelle are suspended in a bubble of bliss. *Please*, he thinks, *nobody pop it.*

He makes a vow silently.

He will be a good husband and an even better father. He will buy a place for the three of them; he will marry Isabelle, and she will get a green card and, hopefully, become an American citizen.

Kevin lays Isabelle carefully down across his bed. He lifts the hem of her Mrs. Claus dress, and starts peppering her stomach with kisses.

She says, "Oh no, Kevin! Everyone is awake!"

"So?" he says.

"So I should be helping to clean."

"Ava will clean up," he says.

"They're going to think you just proposed, and now we are back here..."

He takes one of her braids in his mouth.

"Kevin!" she says. "Stop! Your family just found out about us. I am sure they are still...so shocked."

"Who cares?" he says.

"I care!" Isabelle says. "I am still a worker here. And, listen—it sounds like something is going on."

Kevin tries not to lose his patience. He finally has Isabelle in his bedroom without it having to be a covert mission. She is his fiancée, and he would like to make proper love to her immediately. But he closes his eyes and listens. There does seem to be some kind of ruckus in the main room of the inn.

"Maybe the tree fell over," Kevin says.

"Maybe is Mitzi!" Isabelle says. She hops to her feet, incited by this thought. Kevin knows she would like to give Mitzi a good, sound slap across the face. Mitzi brought Isabelle into the family and then left it herself. "I would like to go out and see."

"Let's not and say we did."

"Kevin," Isabelle says. "It is your family."

"*Our* family," he says, and he's so tickled by this thought that he doesn't even mind following Isabelle out into the hallway.

*   *   *

The main room is freezing because the front door is standing wide open. There is a loud, strange noise like that of a trapped or hurt animal, and Kevin sees his father embracing someone wearing a dark coat. Ava comes rushing out of the kitchen, followed by Scott in his Santa suit.

"Patrick?" Ava says.

Kevin is confused until he realizes that the figure his father is hugging and shushing is indeed the crown prince of the Quinn family. Patrick is *crying,* but to say he's crying doesn't begin to describe it. He's sobbing, bellowing, howling. Kevin hasn't seen this kind of emotion out of his brother since childhood—one scary afternoon at Nobadeer Beach when Patrick was ten and Kevin was nine and a wave took Patrick by surprise. It turned him upside down, inside out, and backward, and then there was another wave on top of that, and then another wave on top of that. Kevin had been too stunned and far too cowardly to make any move to help his brother, although he could see if someone didn't come to the rescue, Patrick was going to drown.

Kelley had run down from where he and Margaret were sitting on the beach, and he pulled Patrick out. Patrick is crying now much as he had cried then—as if his life were in danger.

Ava says, "What…what is *wrong?*"

Isabelle squeezes Kevin's arm and heads back to the kitchen. She is family now, but he can't blame her for not wanting to jump right into this mess. Scott follows Isabelle into the kitchen, so then it's just Kevin and Ava and Patrick and Kelley in the main room, plus a fifth presence, which is Patrick's enormous sadness.

Kevin shuts the front door. He's happy Patrick is here. He can't wait to see the look on Paddy's face when he tells him he's getting married and having a baby.

Ava is standing a few feet away from the melded figures of Patrick and Kelley, looking confused and bereft. She doesn't like being left in the dark; she always has to know what's going on.

"What is *wrong?*" she asks again.

Kevin decides the proper course of action is to pour shots of Jameson all around. They are, after all, a family of Irish heritage, their great-grandfather Quinn hailing from County Cork, so whiskey is acceptable in any emergency. Kevin brings the bottle and four shot glasses over to the sofa and coffee table in front of the hearth. The fireplace is laid out with birch logs as decoration for the party—it's always too hot in the room to light it, plus Mitzi thinks fires lead to inhalation of secondhand smoke—but now Kevin opens the flue and stuffs a bunch of used paper napkins and some kindling under the logs. The room is cold, it's Christmas Eve, they are a family in crisis, and, along with whiskey, they need a fire.

"Come," Kevin says once he gets the fire started. "Sit."

In general, Kevin doesn't have much luck when he tries to tell his family what to do, but tonight his voice is strong and clear and authoritative. Ava sits, and Kelley leads Patrick

143

over, at which point Patrick collapses on his back, hogging most of the room.

Kevin pours the shots and hands them around. Patrick already smells like a distillery and probably needs a shot of Jameson like he needs a hole in the head. He's wearing rumpled suit pants and a white dress shirt with a weird yellow-purple stain on the front. It looks like a bruise. He hasn't shaved in a couple of days. He's not wearing socks, just fancy Italian suede loafers that probably cost as much as Kevin makes in a week.

Kevin raises his shot glass, and the rest of his family follows suit. Kelley takes a breath as if to say something — perhaps to impart some fatherly wisdom, which, Kevin realizes, they all desperately need. It has been *so long* since it's been just the four of them alone doing anything. In Kevin's memory, the four of them haven't been alone together since Kelley moved out of the brownstone and into that weird executive apartment on Wall Street. That was during the year of transition: Margaret was gone, and Mitzi had not yet arrived. Patrick and Kevin and Ava used to take the 2/3 train down to see their father every other weekend, and they would always visit the South Street Seaport because the rest of the financial district was closed up. Once, Kelley took them to Windows on the World, at the top of the World Trade Center. Ten years later, on September 11, all Kevin could think about was that dinner. He and Patrick had stared out the window and wondered if anyone could jump and survive.

No.

They, however, have survived. Sort of.

Kelley seems to realize that there isn't anything wise or even appropriate he can say, and so the four of them merely touch glasses and throw the shots back, then set the glasses back on the table, all of this nearly in unison.

Ava wipes her lips. "I miss Mommy," she says.

This starts Patrick crying again, and for a second Kevin feels like crying, too. For a second, the four of them are nothing more than refugees of something broken that they all wished could be whole again.

KELLEY

Ava heads off to bed first, and shortly after, Isabelle emerges from the kitchen—cleanup is done—and Kevin rises, takes her hand, and leads her to the back of the house.

Kevin and Isabelle are engaged, Kelley thinks. He's both thrilled and incredulous. And they're having a *baby*. He'd always thought Kevin would make a magnificent father, but, after the way Norah Vale left him bruised and bleeding in the gutter, it didn't seem likely. Not unless something astonishing happened.

Such as meeting Isabelle.

Kelley feels like Happy Scrooge again, despite his many troubles. He can't *wait* to share the news with Margaret. Tomorrow, when she calls from Hawaii, he'll get her on the line alone, and they will celebrate the advent of a fourth Quinn grandbaby—a piece of each of them coming together in another human being.

Kelley misses Mitzi; that hurt is fresh and new, like a bad toothache. But he misses Margaret, too, differently, in an older way, like a bone that has broken and never been set properly.

And Kelley misses Bart. That hurt is like a thorn in the soft arch of his foot that he valiantly tries to ignore. He wonders if Bart will be allowed to call home on Christmas.

But now isn't the time to worry about Kevin or Bart. It's time to worry about Patrick. Kelley can't remember a single other time when Patrick has sought advice or counsel, when Patrick has come to him crying in pain or shame. He was born knowing what to do—he slept through the night, he crawled early, he walked early, he started reading early, he was valedictorian of his class, he got in early decision at Colgate, then got into Harvard Business School, and, in a handful of years, was made head of private equity at Everlast Investments. He married the right girl, bought the right house, fathered three noisy, beautiful sons. He is just like Margaret, Kelley thinks, in the way he seamlessly pursues exactly what he wants and gets it. Kelley was more like that before, when he lived in New York and was basically single-handedly responsible for setting the price of gasoline in the United States. Of course, Kelley wasn't a very nice person back then, and he suspects that Patrick isn't always very nice, either. The other kids think he's a relentless bastard.

But here he is, on the sofa with Kelley, as bereft as a sixteen-year-old girl who lost her prom date.

Kelley gives Patrick what he thinks is ample time to explain on his own what the problem is, but Paddy says nothing and it's getting late and it is Christmas Eve, and Kelley has endured one hell of a day and a half. The conversation he had in the master bedroom with George seems like three years ago.

"What happened, Paddy?" Kelley asks softly.

"I screwed up," Patrick says. "Like, really badly."

Kelley assumes he means he cheated on Jennifer—which is the only reason Kelley can think of for why Jen and his grandsons aren't here. Kelley feels a piercing disappointment in his son. Kelley is no saint, not by a long shot, but he was never unfaithful to either of his wives. He's not built like that, though he knows many men are. He's surprised at Patrick because he thought Paddy and Jen were one of those couples destined for forever. They adore and respect each other, and they're best friends, besides. They finish each other's sentences. Jen has found a career that dovetails with her role as wife and mother; Kelley has some notion that it's easier for women to balance home and career now than it was when Margaret was trying to do it.

"Jen is…?" Kelley asks, hoping Patrick will say she's still in Boston; that way, reconciliation by morning and a chance for Kelley to see his grandsons are both still possible.

"In San Francisco," Patrick says. "She took the kids to her mother's."

Kelley is crushed. "Oh."

"She's really disappointed in me," Patrick says. "And afraid of what's going to happen. Our financial future."

Kelley wonders if Patrick did something really stupid and got some girl pregnant.

"Patrick," Kelley says, "what happened?"

Patrick takes a deep breath, and it all spills out: He tells first about the perks he's been taking from clients over the years, and then about his Colgate reunion and the conversation with Bucky Larimer, and Bucky's reassurance that the drug would be approved by the FDA and would change the face of childhood leukemia and possibly of all cancers, and then about Bucky's request that in exchange for this information Patrick invest money for Bucky himself, his identity obfuscated by a trust. Patrick goes on, telling about how he was feeling giddy about a bright medical future for mankind, but also *greedy greedy greedy,* so he poured $23.6 million of his clients' portfolios into Panagea. The good news is that the drug *will* be FDA approved; the bad news is that Patrick's investments with Panagea were red-flagged by the SEC. The SEC had been scrutinizing him because of the perks. They have a watch list for people they suspect are weak of character.

"Doesn't everyone in the business take perks?" Kelley asks. "Isn't that the way the industry works?" The same was certainly true in Kelley's day, and, honestly, it was probably worse back then—in the era of the pin-striped suit and the power tie, the age of *Wall Street,* Ivan Boesky, and Michael Milken.

"Apparently my perks were 'excessive,'" Patrick says. "The SEC had me on this watch list, and my compliance department knew it, but they didn't tell me. I was basically stung by my own guys! Nobody really likes Compliance; I mean, we all work toward the same bottom line, but we don't invite them into the football pool or anything. They were waiting around for me to do something they could really nail me on." Patrick wipes his nose with the back of his hand. Kelley wishes he carried a handkerchief, like George. Instead, he hands Patrick a damp cocktail napkin. "And they were right, I did." He starts crying again, but more quietly; he is whimpering. Kelley puts a hand around Patrick's ankle and thinks there is nothing he can say, and nothing he can do except hold on.

AVA

She is drunk. Drunk, drunk, drunk, teetering in her high heels, which she kicks off sky-high in her bedroom. She falls onto her bed. Should she check her phone?

She has the spins. She sits up. That last shot of Jameson did her in. Goddamned Kevin and Patrick. They suck. All boys suck. She gets to her feet. She needs ice water and something to eat—one of the snowflake rolls she was planning on serving tomorrow, or some crackers. She careens down the hallway, through the back entrance to the kitchen.

She nearly screams. Santa Claus is sitting at the counter, picking at the remains of the ham. At first, Ava feels a sense of childish wonder—Santa! In the kitchen, on Christmas Eve, just as she always imagined! But then she realizes that it's Scott. He has a jar of mustard out, and he's smearing the pieces of ham before he eats them.

He sees her but seems unsurprised and unashamed to be in the Quinns' kitchen after everyone else has gone to bed.

"Hey," he says.

"Are there any little biscuits left?" she asks. "Or tiny slices of pumpernickel?"

"Long gone," he says.

"I need ice water," Ava says. "And maybe some crackers. I'm pretty drunk."

Scott fetches Ava a glass of ice water and finds an entire box of Carr's rosemary crackers, Ava's favorite. She takes a second to appreciate a man who will do the small things for her. She smiles at him, or at least she thinks she's smiling at him; she can't feel her face.

Scott misreads her smile for something else. He leans down and kisses Ava, and she finds herself kissing him back. She wonders if she's standing under mistletoe—as a rule, when she sees mistletoe at the inn or in the faculty lounge at school, she takes it down immediately—but she soon forgets about mistletoe, because kissing Scott is unexpectedly... awesome. There's a charge. She is turned on. Is this real, or is it the Jameson? She had been so jealous when she saw Isabelle slip her arm around Scott's shoulders. She's happy it's her kissing Scott right now. They keep going, kissing and kissing, lips and tongues, and teeth—he bites her gently, and electricity runs up her spine. He pulls her in closer; she is now locked against him. She thinks, *This is Scott Skyler, the assistant principal.* Can they have sexual chemistry, despite the fact that she doesn't have romantic feelings for him? Is this even possible? Then Ava thinks of Nathaniel, and she imagines how she would feel if he were kissing Kirsten Cabot the way she is now kissing Scott Skyler.

She pulls away.

"Damn," Scott says. He takes a deep breath. He looks down at himself. "North Pole."

Ava backs up.

"You felt something, right? Something good? Please tell me you felt something good."

She can't speak. She did feel something good, but how cruel to lead Scott on when her emotional state doesn't match her physical state. She picks up the water and the box of crackers. If Shelby were here right now, she would call Ava an asshat.

"Good night," she says. Her lips are buzzing with the tang of mustard. "Merry Christmas."

"Merry Christmas," Scott says weakly.

Ava scurries for the door, thinking she has to get to her bedroom, she has to go to sleep, before anything else happens. But in the doorway, she turns around.

"Scott?" she says.

"Yes?" he says, hopefully.

"Will you come to dinner tomorrow night? Five o'clock? Please? I'm making a standing rib roast and Yorkshire pudding."

He nods but doesn't look happy. "I'll be here," he says.

"Good," she says, and she means it. She needs people other than her family at the table tomorrow. As she heads back to her room, however, she realizes she never made it to the store to pick up the standing rib roast she ordered. Will the store be open on Christmas? If not, they will all have to eat hot dogs from Cumberland Farms. Beef *hot dogs!* Ava thinks.

*   *   *

Once in her room, Ava checks her phone. There is nothing from NO—no missed call, no texts. Ava blinks and feels her heart plummet like a skinny Santa through a chimney. Nothing, not one word. Ava checks her texts and her call log, just to be sure.

Nothing.

She can't help herself. She calls Nathaniel's number and thinks, *Pick up, pick up!* Maybe he, like Ava, got drunk on too much of Mrs. Cabot's eggnog and passed out while dialing Ava's number.

She is treated to Nathaniel's voice mail just after the first ring. Which means his phone is off. He shut off his phone without calling or texting her. Or saying *Merry Christmas.*

Ava climbs underneath her comforter. She is still in her black dress, but she is too tired, and too heartbroken, to take it off.

In the middle of the night, Ava feels arms wrap around her. At first, she worries that Scott has lingered around and crawled into bed with her. Then she thinks, *It's not Scott, it's Nathaniel! He came back!*

But it is neither Scott nor Nathaniel.

It is someone else.

MARGARET

Because she is "Margaret Quinn," the following things happen: She climbs into the car and tells Raoul to take her to Teterboro instead of Newark. Raoul has been driving for Margaret for fifteen years and has never once gotten flustered.

He says, "Teterboro it is."

There is hellacious traffic at the Lincoln Tunnel. Margaret tries not to panic; she tries not to *think*. Second-guessing herself never works.

She calls Lee Kramer, the head of the network. He's Jewish, so she's not too worried about interrupting his Christmas Eve. But, as it turns out, he's at a holiday party at EN, in the West Village, and it sounds like he's had a few too many sakes. Margaret hopes this works to her advantage.

Lee says, "Great broadcast tonight. Ginny thinks you look great in red."

Ginny, Lee's wife, is an editor at *Vogue,* so Margaret can't really object.

"Thank you," she says. Then, "Lee, I need a huge favor."

"For you," he says, "anything."

Right. Because she has done more than her share of huge favors for him. She has traveled to the epicenters of floods and earthquakes and tsunamis; she has stood before the wreckage of horrific plane crashes and school shootings. She has reported the news, grim though it has tended to be, without complaining.

"I need one of the jets at Teterboro and a pilot. The smallest jet; it's just me."

"To go to *Hawaii?*" Lee asks.

"No, no, I had to cancel Hawaii," Margaret says. "I'm going to Nantucket instead. To be with my kids."

"Oh, okay," Lee says. "Much closer. I'll call Ned and see what he has. When do you need it?"

Margaret eyes the traffic. "In an hour?"

"Oh boy," Lee says. "You do know it's Christmas Eve, right? You might have better luck calling St. Nick and hitching a ride on the sleigh." He laughs heartily. "I just made a Christmas joke. Me, a kid from Livingston, New Jersey. The rabbi would be so proud."

"Lee?" Margaret says. "I really need this. It's for my children."

"Give me ten minutes," Lee says. "Ned will call you directly."

"Thank you," Margaret says. "You're a mensch."

"That I am," Lee says, and he hangs up.

Margaret sighs deeply. Raoul says, "You okay, Maggie?"

Only Raoul—and Kelley—call her Maggie. She smiles. "Hanging in." She hates to tell Raoul that if she can't fly to Nantucket tonight, she'll have to ask him to drive her up to Hyannis. But no—she can't do that to Raoul on Christmas

Eve. She knows he always goes to midnight Mass with his granddaughter, who is a student at Hunter College. So Margaret will have to rent a car and drive herself to Hyannis, spend the night at the DoubleTree, then fly over to the island first thing in the morning.

Good-bye, Maui; good-bye, Drake; good-bye, hot-stone massage.

Then Margaret chastises herself. Bart was most likely on that convoy and is now being held prisoner somewhere in Afghanistan. *Kelley Kelley Kelley Kelley Kelley Kelley*—his son, his baby. Margaret has to get to him.

Stuck.

In.

Traffic.

Where are all these souls *going* on Christmas Eve? Why aren't they at home with their families?

Margaret digs into her luggage—the bikinis and cover-ups and sandals and straw hat have all been rendered useless—until she finds the zipped pocket where she stashed Ava's paper angel. She lays the paper angel in her lap. She was raised Catholic and educated by the nuns, but her faith has morphed greatly over the years—it has both faltered and deepened. She is more certain now than ever that there is something bigger out there, but she is less sure what it is. God? Allah? Karma?

Holding the paper angel on her lap brings back the best

memories, but only in snippets. The first Christmas with Paddy, when he was just a newborn. Margaret set him under the tree in his Moses basket, and neither she nor Kelley bought each other any gifts that year, because what could be more perfect than the gift they had created together?

The year she and Kelley drove from Manhattan to Kelley's mother's house, in Perrysburg, Ohio, through a blinding snowstorm, with Patrick and Kevin strapped into car seats in the back. Margaret was convinced they'd get stranded; she made Kelley promise they would never again leave Manhattan at the holidays, and they never had.

The string of years in the brownstone. There were some good memories, before Margaret's career took off, back when she actually had time for things. Margaret used to pick the kids up from school and ogle all the shopwindows and then take them up to the seventh floor of Bergdorf's for hot chocolate. She made sugar cookies every year with Ava: colored icing, silver balls, green and red jimmies. Kelley's firm used to throw a whopper of a holiday party at Le Cirque — oysters and champagne and a twenty-two-piece orchestra, everyone drunk, partners' wives doing lines of cocaine in the bathroom while wearing their furs. That had been the last rush of big-time Reagan-era prosperity — life before cell phones and the Internet. Margaret had a certain nostalgia for that time, those parties, the big hair. Patrick and Kevin used to participate in the pageant at their church on Eighty-Eighth Street. They were usually shepherds, but one year

Patrick was picked to be Joseph, and Kelley and Margaret were given seats in the front pew. Margaret loved the pageant, with its menagerie of barn animals and little children dressed as angels, and the whole sanctuary bathed in candlelight. The organist would play "O Come, All Ye Faithful," and the church walls would practically swell with the voices, young and old.

Christmas Eve—always quiche lorraine and spinach salad with hot bacon dressing, and a viewing of the movie where the little boy wants a BB gun. Margaret and Kelley would drink Golden Dreams and get pleasantly mulled before putting the kids to bed and setting out the presents.

It had all been a golden dream, Margaret thought. If only they had realized it at the time.

Margaret's phone rings. It's Ned, who is in charge of the four network-owned jets.

"Margaret," he says, "I have one plane with crew ready to go, but I have to remind you, it's meant for urgent scenarios. You know, for news stories. Lee okayed it, so I'm going to let it slide tonight, but this can't become a habit."

"It won't ever happen again," Margaret says, wishing Lee had told Ned to spare her the lecture. "I promise."

"Anyway, the problem is that Nantucket is closing its airport at nine. I can contact them, but I'm warning you, the likelihood that they're going to stay open for you on

Christmas Eve is pretty low." He clears his throat. "People want to get home."

I want to get home, Margaret thinks. By no stretch of the imagination is Nantucket Island her home, although she and Kelley started going there in the summer years when the kids were small. They used to rent a house on North Liberty Street that had a screened-in porch, a charcoal grill, and no TV. It had been the perfect place to unplug, unwind, and watch the boys and Ava play endless games of badminton in the side yard. When Margaret and Kelley split, Kelley "got" Nantucket; Margaret is now just a visitor. But her children are there, and this makes it the closest thing to a home that Margaret has.

"Please check, Ned," Margaret says. "Please. Tell the tower that once I'm on the ground, I'll sign autographs. I'll do photos. I'll write their kids college recommendations."

"Okay," Ned says, and he hangs up.

Raoul pops in Margaret's favorite CD by the Vienna Boys' Choir. She leans back and wonders briefly what Drake is doing. She assumes he'll go to Hawaii alone. He will meet someone else—a young divorcée or one of the luscious college-dropout bartenders. He will lose the intellectual stimulation that Margaret brings, but he will gain youth and vigor in bed. She can't even summon the energy to text him, though she wishes him well.

Her phone rings. It's Ned. *Bad news,* she thinks. It's a

five-hour drive to Hyannis (does she even remember *how* to drive?). She will get to the DoubleTree at two a.m. If she's lucky.

"You're not going to believe this," Ned says. "The secretary of state is flying in at midnight tonight from Israel, so Nantucket airspace is open until then!" He sounds truly joyous, as if nothing makes him happier than delivering Margaret this Christmas miracle. "When can you get here?"

Margaret feels the car surge forward. The traffic has just cleared, and Raoul steps on it.

"Half an hour," she says. "I'm on my way."

KELLEY

George was the one who always wore the red suit, but Kelley is the real Santa Claus at the Quinn household.

Despite everything that's happened, Kelley stuffs the stockings—he even stuffs stockings for Patrick's three boys, as if by some reverse Christmas magic, the presents will make them appear. He puts gifts for everyone under the tree.

He checks his phone, but there is no word from Bart.

It is Christmas morning in Afghanistan.

Kelley goes to bed.

DECEMBER 25

MARGARET

She wakes up with her daughter snuggled at her side. Margaret is filled with such joy, she nearly cries. Her career has come at an enormous cost, and the person who has suffered the most, she knows, is Ava. Ava was only six years old when Margaret and Kelley split and ten when Kelley moved to Nantucket. Margaret had considered keeping Ava with her in Manhattan—even at six, she demonstrated an exceptional musical talent, and the best place to develop that was in the city. But Ava would have been raised by house-keepers and nannies, whereas Kelley had given up every-thing to be a hands-on parent, and Margaret had reluctantly agreed that Ava would be better off with him. Still, six years old is a tender age for a girl to be separated from her mother. Margaret always told herself she was leading by example, building a legendary career. She had thought Ava would be a concert pianist or perhaps a rock star. But Ava likes teaching music on Nantucket, and Margaret is happy she is happy. Now she hopes that Ava will find true love, get married, have children, and be the mother that Margaret never was.

Ava opens her eyes, blinking rapidly in the way she used to when she was young, except now her eyes are smudged with makeup and she's wearing a black velvet cocktail dress. The party the night before must have been a humdinger.

Margaret thinks about the captured convoy, and Bart. She has found herself in many delicate situations before, but nothing has quite prepared her for what to do here. She doesn't know for sure that Bart was on the convoy; it's just a gut feeling. However, her gut is nearly always right. Should she share her knowledge with Ava? With Kevin? With Kelley? If she's wrong this time, she'll never forgive herself. But if she's right, everyone will hate her, despite the fact that she is merely the messenger.

She decides to say nothing. Once there is definitive news, military officials will contact Kelley.

"Mommy?" Ava says. "Are you real?"

"I'm real," Margaret says.

She and Ava cling to each other and Margaret cries a little and Ava cries a little and Margaret can't decide whether to feel heroic for being here or guilty for all the days she wasn't here.

"I decided, since I couldn't get you to Hawaii, that I would come here instead," Margaret says. "I wanted to be with you."

"Thank you, Mommy," Ava says.

"And look!" Margaret says. She points to the nightstand. "I brought your paper angel."

"Let's hope she really is magic," Ava says.

"How are things with Nathaniel?" Margaret asks.

"He doesn't love me," Ava says.

Deep breath. This happens, Margaret knows. You can give birth to a beautiful, perfect human being, but requited love isn't guaranteed for her—or for any of us.

Margaret wonders for a second if Drake is feeling anything this morning. Did she *hurt* him by canceling? Is he heartsick?

Margaret kisses the tip of Ava's nose. "Should we go make coffee?" Margaret wants to see Kevin, and Kelley. "Your father doesn't know I'm here. Nobody does. I'm basically a stowaway."

Ava clings tighter. "Don't get up yet. Stay just mine for now, please?"

Margaret relaxes, then nearly falls asleep. She is exhausted in every way, just as she is every Christmas—physically, mentally, emotionally. For the first time in 360 days, her laptop is uncharged in the front pocket of her carry-on. When she stepped off the plane the night before, she found the secretary of state and his wife waiting for her. Margaret felt flattered by this—not only because it was the secretary of state, but because John and Teresa are friends from way back. Margaret interviewed him during his first run for senator, in

1984, when she was a graduate student in communications at NYU.

The secretary said, "Where are you headed?"

She said, "The Winter Street Inn. My ex-husband, Kelley, owns it."

He said, "That's right, that's right. My driver will take you."

"Wonderful," she said.

Margaret has nothing packed that is even remotely appropriate for Nantucket in December, and so she borrows a T-shirt and sweatpants from Ava and pulls on her own pink Chanel cardigan.

Ava says, "I'm going to sleep a little while longer. The kids aren't here, so it doesn't matter."

"What happened with Paddy?" Margaret asks.

Ava gives Margaret a look. "He got himself in trouble, I guess."

"What kind of trouble?"

"He'll tell you himself," Ava says. "He's here."

"He *is?*" Margaret says, and before Ava even makes a face, Margaret knows she sounds like a starstruck teenager. It is a long-held family complaint that both Margaret and Kelley favor Patrick. Margaret vehemently denies this, although there is something special about Patrick. He was the first, obviously, and his whole life has been a clinic in How to Excel.

He got himself in trouble. What could this mean?

Margaret bends down and kisses her sleepy daughter's forehead; then she heads out into the hallway to find the rest of her family.

She walks toward the kitchen and the smell of coffee. She's nervous, almost like she's doing something illegal. Every other time she's been at the inn, she's had to deal with Mitzi's wrath.

But Mitzi isn't here, Margaret reminds herself. If Mitzi *were* here, Margaret would be in Hawaii. Margaret wonders if any of the guests will pop their heads out of their rooms to find Margaret Quinn roaming the hallway. Her photo is bound to end up on Twitter.

In the great room, Margaret is greeted by the tree, under which lie mounds and mounds of presents. The battalion of Mitzi's nutcrackers lines the mantel; Margaret has only been to the inn at Christmas once before, a dozen years earlier, but she remembers the nutcrackers well. Her favorite is the gardener nutcracker, with his rake, watering can, and green overalls. Margaret runs her hand over the slanted top of Ava's grand piano, and then, unable to help herself, she lifts the lid off of a glass apothecary jar and pulls out a piece of green, white, and hot-pink striped ribbon candy and takes a lick.

When Margaret enters the kitchen, Kelley is by himself, drinking coffee at the counter. Margaret feels a rush of what must be love—the kind of love one feels for a brother, perhaps, or a long-lost best friend. She knows the man *so well,* better than she knows anyone else on earth, including her own children, and yet she hasn't lived with him in more than two decades and has only seen him fleetingly when she's come to visit Nantucket in August, and every one of those interactions was supervised by Mitzi.

"Kelley," she says.

He looks up and blinks.

"Are you real?" he says.

"I'm real," she says.

Where to start? Where to start? They hug, long and hard. Kelley smells like himself, which is Irish on Irish—Irish Spring soap and Irish whiskey.

She pulls away first, as she always does—that much intimacy crosses some kind of line with Margaret, which in some ways caused the downfall of their marriage. Kelley always wanted more, closer, tighter—and Margaret wanted space and boundaries. She was afraid of intimacy, Kelley said. Margaret called it Retaining a Sense of Self. She never believed in two people melding to become one. She believed in self-sufficiency. After all, everyone dies alone.

"How's Bart?" she asks gently. "Have you heard from him?"

"He texted when he left Germany," Kelley says. "But I haven't heard from him since."

"When was that?" Margaret asks.

"The night of the nineteenth," Kelley says. "I'm sure he's either too busy, or the reception is nonexistent. I'm surprised I heard from him at all."

Margaret's heart feels like a vessel filled to the brim with some potentially toxic liquid. Is she going to spill it? She knows nothing for certain, and until the military gets in touch, there is no cause for alarm.

Her gut tells her otherwise.

But it's Christmas morning, so she will ignore her gut.

"Is there coffee?" she asks.

"Yes! Of course!" Kelley jumps right into innkeeper mode, the consummate host. He fetches a cup of cinnamon-flavored coffee in a thick ceramic mug decorated with a raised set of crisscrossed candy canes, and then he presents her with a plate of dark-brown muffins.

"Pumpkin ginger," he says. "I baked them myself."

Margaret sips her cinnamon-flavored coffee, trying not to wince—she drinks espresso only, the more hot and bitter, the better—but it's actually pretty good. She abandons her ribbon candy—it looks a lot better than it tastes—and takes a muffin, despite the fact that she never eats breakfast, and Kelley gives her a ramekin of honey butter. This is life at a bed-and-breakfast: the homey atmosphere, the fresh-baked muffins, the colonial decor of the kitchen. If she were being cynical, she would say it's sort of like being suspended in a Thomas Kinkade painting, but she appreciates how cozy and rustic the room and the inn in general feel; it appeals to her childhood fantasy of Christmas. Margaret's taste is generally sleeker and more sophisticated; her apartment in New York is spacious, and it has forever views across Central Park — but cozy it is not.

"So," she says between bites of fragrant, moist, buttery muffin, "what's up with our eldest?"

"Insider trading," Kelley says. "He invested over twenty-five million in a leukemia drug he knew was going to score. He got word from one of his fraternity brothers and invested that guy's money and everyone else's...and it looks like he got caught. The SEC has been watching him, apparently, because of some other stuff."

Margaret says, "Insider trading."

Kelley nods, and they lock eyes.

"With the dissemination of information these days, I can't believe that term even still exists," Margaret says. "Isn't it sort of like smoking pot? Too prevalent to effectively prosecute?"

"Apparently not."

"Twenty-five million isn't so much money," Margaret says. She realizes her maternal instincts are overriding her moral compass. She, after all, has reported on Kenneth Lay and Enron, Lehman Brothers, Bear Stearns, and the big winner...Bernie Madoff. Until this second, she had liked nothing better than a good financial scandal. "I mean, it could have been much worse. I'm surprised the SEC even noticed."

"They noticed."

"It's not our fault," Margaret says. "So stop thinking that."

"I'm not thinking that," Kelley says. "Are *you* thinking that?"

"No," Margaret says. But yes, she is. It's the curse of any parent, isn't it? When your child has a crack in his character, you feel responsible. Patrick was always such a straight arrow, an ardent follower of the rules. He loved rules.

"He's thirty-eight years old," Kelley says. "That's when men get greedy. His kids are getting older, he starts thinking about how much boarding school is going to cost, then college. He wants a Jaguar; Jen wants a summer house on Cliff Road so they don't have to keep staying here at the inn. Here's an easy way for him to pocket five or six million himself, plus make a boatload of profit for his clients, who will then invest even more money with him. I can see where it would have been tempting."

"He's here?"

"Here," Kelley confirms. "Jen took the kids to San Francisco."

"Ouch."

"And in other, happier news," Kelley says, "Kevin is getting married. He proposed last night to Isabelle, my girl Friday. None of us even knew they were seeing each other. And she's pregnant."

"I know," Margaret says. "I gave him five thousand dollars so he could buy the ring."

Kelley gets a look on his face, and Margaret says, "Don't."

"Don't what?"

"Don't make that *face*," Margaret says. "Like I trumped you again, or like I'm always giving the kids handouts to make up for the fact that I almost never see them."

"I wasn't thinking that," Kelley says.

"What were you thinking, then?"

"I was thinking, can you lend me four million dollars so I don't lose the inn?"

"Are you going to lose the inn?" Margaret asks.

"I have to sell it," Kelley says. "You'll notice there's nobody here? Not one paying guest at the Winter Street Inn on Christmas. The bed-and-breakfast market is all dried up on Nantucket. People can stay at the White Elephant or down the street at the Castle for about the same price, and I can't compete. And this place has gobbled up all my savings. Now I'm nearly broke, and Mitzi left anyway, so I have no desire to prostrate myself at the foot of some loan officer to borrow against the equity. I'm sixty-two years old, and I'm all alone."

"Stop the pity party," Margaret says. "You're not alone. You have the kids. And today, you have me."

Kelley beams. "Today I have you! Would you like to come back to my bedroom and see my etchings?"

Margaret laughs. "The pathetic thing is that, yes, I would."

"Really?" Kelley says, raising his eyebrows.

"I'm pretty lonely," Margaret says. "And I blew off the man I was meeting in Hawaii so I could show up here and save the day."

"Well, then!" Kelley says. He takes Margaret by the hand, but she breaks free.

"I'll be there in a minute," she says. She wants to use Ava's bathroom to freshen up.

"Be quick," Kelley says. "The kids are going to wake up eventually."

The kids, Margaret thinks.

Is she really going to do this? Sleep with Kelley?

She brushes her teeth, applies the moisturizer that Roger claims can fix anything, smiles at her reflection in the mirror. She looks a decade older than she does on TV—no surprise there—makeup, lighting, television magic. Should she put on mascara or concealer? No. Kelley won't care if she's wearing makeup or not. He's seen her after giving birth, for God's sake—three times. And he always said that was the most beautiful she ever looked.

Sweet man.

So…she's fifty-nine years old, and she's about to have sex with her ex-husband.

Really?

Really. She's old enough to have learned that sex is just sex, and at fifty-nine and sixty-two, desire should be treated like a rare and precious commodity. She's also grateful that forgiveness and the passing of time have brought them to this moment.

She sneaks down the hall, toward the master bedroom— quickly, quietly, so as not to wake her children.

PATRICK

He wakes up with the headache of a lifetime, but someone has thoughtfully left a giant glass of ice water and a bottle of Advil by his bed. Patrick drinks down the water, and it tastes so good and so cold, and his body needs it so badly, that he decides to start his day feeling grateful.

He checks his phone. Four missed calls late last night from the temporary cell phone of Bucky Larimer and a text from that number that says, *Dude, call me.* A missed call from Gary Grimstead.

Nothing from Jennifer, which he can't believe. They have never gone this long without speaking—not ever. He feels like his right side is missing. He can make it through anything as long as she is next to him. He closes his eyes and thinks about her. What is she doing right now? Well, it's three hours earlier in California, so she's sleeping. But maybe not. It's nearly ten o'clock here, meaning seven o'clock there, so everyone is probably awake. The boys are opening presents from Santa Claus and from Grammie. Jennifer's mother is wealthy and always too lavish; the boys might not even miss the ten million presents that remain under the tree in Boston, or the presents here for them on Nantucket. Jennifer will be drinking coffee, maybe with a splash of Baileys in it, trying to put on a brave face. They will go to the Park Tavern for brunch because Jennifer's mother doesn't cook.

Patrick dislikes that part of the San Francisco tradition — who goes *out* on Christmas morning?

He resists the urge to call Jennifer. She probably won't answer anyway.

He needs coffee, more water, food. He made it from Boston to Hyannis in forty-eight minutes, getting his BMW up to 110 miles per hour on Route 3, which probably would have landed him in jail sooner than he's already going, but for the fact that the road was free of troopers. Patrick missed one ferry; then he started drinking at the Naked Oyster and missed two more ferries before finally getting on the seven o'clock. He drank Sam Adams on the boat, and then he walked up Main Street to the inn, stopping at Murray's Liquors and buying and consuming a split of Taittinger champagne on the way. Once here, he was welcomed into the bosom of his family and offered a shot of Jameson.

Patrick stands up. He spent the night in Bart's room, which is still filled with Bart's paraphernalia, including a large purple bong — a bag of weed was easily found in Bart's underwear drawer — car magazines, a poster of Lindsay Lohan on the wall.

Lindsay Lohan? Patrick thinks. He's relieved Bart has joined the Marines. Anyone who publicly announces himself a fan of Lindsay Lohan needs straightening out.

Tucked into Bart's mirror are ticket stubs from the Patriots-Broncos game this past October. Kelley probably took him up to Foxborough for it before he shipped out to Germany. Kelley was a good, involved dad like that for Bart.

Patrick steps out into the hallway, and he hears giggling. He turns around to see Kelley and a redheaded woman emerging from Kelley's room.

Whoa! Patrick thinks. He squints at the redhead. His mind isn't quite clear, but it looks like his mother. It *is* his mother. She sees him, and her mouth falls open.

"Are you real?" Patrick asks.

"I'm real," she says.

KELLEY

He's not sure how this happened, but Christmas is everything it's supposed to be and more. To start with, Kelley makes love to his ex-wife. Mitzi was never interested in sex at Christmas—of course, now Kelley knows that's because for the past twelve years, she was having sex with George.

The lovemaking with Margaret is easy and comfortable and familiar—you forget, but you never really forget. Kelley does the things that Margaret likes, and she does the things that he likes. Afterward, they lie next to each other, sweating and breathless, staring up at the ceiling.

"I read in *Esquire* magazine that sixty percent of American males over fifty fantasize about sleeping with you,"

Kelley says. "But seventy-five percent fantasize about sleeping with Martha Stewart. I never really understood that. Maybe because she can cook?"

Margaret clobbers him with a pillow, and soon the two of them are laughing and wrestling and tickling each other. Margaret is ticklish behind her knees; her laughter soon turns to screams for mercy. Kelley stops because she is making so much noise. It's a delightful, juvenile hour, the greatest gift he ever could have hoped for.

A big, happy reunion follows. Patrick sees Margaret first— he catches her coming out of Kelley's bedroom—and he throws her over his shoulder and carries her out to the main room. Kevin and Isabelle wander out, and Kevin gives a whoop and picks Margaret up off the ground also.

She says, "I haven't been picked up and thrown around this much since my cheerleading days at Michigan."

Kelley says, "You weren't a cheerleader at Michigan."

"Let me have my fantasies," she says.

"I thought that's what I just did," Kelley says.

Ava emerges from the back. She slept with Margaret the night before, but she looks grumpy now at having to share her.

Kelley lights a fire and enlists Kevin to make a batch of Golden Dreams. If they're going to have a nostalgic Quinn Family Christmas, then they are going whole hog.

Kevin says, "I know you and Mom used to drink them, but I have no idea what goes into one."

Kevin looks to Margaret. "What's in a Golden Dream?"

177

Margaret is curled up on the sofa with a dazed look that Kelley hopes is postcoital bliss.

"Galliano, Cointreau, orange juice, and cream," she says.

The woman forgets nothing, Kelley thinks. She is the smartest human being he has ever met.

Kevin nods. "On it."

Ava says, "I dropped the ball on Christmas dinner. I ordered the rib roast, but I forgot to go pick it up. And now I'm sure the store is closed."

"I picked it up yesterday," Isabelle says. "They called with a reminder, so I went to get it."

"Oh, thank you!" Ava says.

"In a little while, I'll help you prepare it," Margaret says. "Are we having Yorkshire pudding?"

"Of course," Ava says. "And roasted asparagus and spinach salad."

"I'll do my hot bacon dressing for the salad," Margaret says.

"What man in his right mind would rather sleep with Martha Stewart?" Kelley says.

They all drink and open presents. One person opens at a time—Quinn family tradition, so that it lasts longer. It's admittedly easier to accomplish this without the grandchildren around. Patrick's boys are ten-, eight-, and six-year-old weapons of mass destruction. The other person who never obeyed present-opening protocol was Bart. Even in his late teens, he would come down and rip open all his presents at once.

Mitzi never reprimanded him, of course.

The year they gave him a brand-new Jeep Sahara in metallic royal blue with a massive silver ribbon wrapped around it counts as the worst Christmas on record. Bart was thrilled; he was straight out of central casting, a seventeen-year-old kid jumping up and down, hooting and hollering, hugging Mitzi, hugging Kelley, saying *Oh man, oh man, you guys rock!* Ava, Kevin, and Patrick, however, had stared at the Jeep in disbelief. None of them had said a word, but Kelley heard their thoughts.

A brand-new Jeep for a seventeen-year-old kid who hasn't made the honor roll since sixth grade, who smashed up the last car—Mitzi's Volvo station wagon—so that all it was good for was the demolition derby, a kid who you know drinks and smokes dope. You're giving HIM a brand-new Jeep, when none of us got so much as a new bicycle?

Kelley hadn't wanted to give Bart the Jeep, but Mitzi insisted. She believed that if Bart was given something he really loved and treasured, he would take care of it, thereby learning an important lesson about responsibility.

Bart drove the Jeep into Miacomet Pond in June, and the water was brackish enough that the engine block seized.

Totaled.

Then, five months later, he did the number on Kelley and Mitzi's LR3, busting a hole in the airport fence and breaking his best friend's leg.

No wonder Kelley is going broke.

How can Mitzi possibly argue that Bart did not need the Marines?

The Christmas of the Jeep—two years earlier—Patrick, Kevin, and Ava gave Kelley and Mitzi the silent treatment all throughout Christmas dinner, leaving poor Jennifer to make chitchat with Mitzi, Kelley, and Bart. Oh, and George, Kelley remembers now; of course George was there. They all ate the goose Mitzi had prepared, which had been unusually stringy that year.

Kelley doesn't want to dwell on the less-than-stellar Christmases of the past; nor does he want to beat himself up for his parenting mistakes. What parent *doesn't* screw up every once in a while?

Patrick gets a tie and a biography of Alexander Hamilton.

Kevin gets a series of boxes within boxes that ends in an envelope of cash—five hundred dollars (in years past it has been a thousand dollars, but Kelley can only do what he can do)—and everyone laughs because this trick, presents nested like Russian dolls, is tradition. It's followed by the requisite remembering of the year Kevin gave Patrick a box of extra-large condoms and Ava, only eleven years old at the time, didn't know what they were.

Then it's Kelley's turn to open his gift from Margaret. It's a small box; he knows what it is, as she gets him the same thing every year. In previous years, he's opened his gift from Margaret privately, all by himself in the quiet of his bedroom, while Mitzi was busy with other things (busy with George, Kelley now realizes), because Mitzi does not appreciate that Margaret still sends him a gift.

"What can it be?" Kelley asks, and Margaret gives her low, throaty chuckle, known to all her faithful viewers.

It's a beautifully tied fly, even more gorgeous than the ones from the past. Margaret once interviewed the foremost saltwater fly fisherman in the world; he lives in Islamorada, and now this guy makes one fly a year for Kelley. The fly is to go with the fly-fishing rod that Margaret bought for Kelley the last Christmas they were still together, back when they vowed to spend less time at work and more time having fun. Kelley had gotten Margaret a mask, fins, and snorkel, which he is certain she has never used, just as he has never used his fly-fishing rod.

But wait.

Not true.

He actually *did* use the rod once, on a warm, still day in September sixteen or seventeen years earlier, but he caught such hell from Mitzi about taking an *entire afternoon to himself* when they had a *three-year-old* and an *inn under construction* that Kelley never went fly-fishing again. Blissfully unaware of this, Margaret keeps giving him a fly every Christmas; he has a box of them in the back of his sock drawer. When viewed together, they are as colorful and exquisite as the crown jewels.

"Thank you," Kelley says, and he leans over to kiss Margaret chastely, as everyone is watching.

Maybe in his retirement: fly-fishing.

Ava gets a sweater.

Patrick gets another tie.

Kevin gets new running shoes.

Kelley gets a whisk and a new potato peeler of good, sturdy Danish design.

Margaret has an envelope to open that is from "the kids" (meaning Ava procured it, Patrick paid for it, and Kevin signed his name to the card). It's two tickets to see *The Book of Mormon,* tenth-row orchestra seats. Margaret claps her hands with delight and kisses each of the kids, and Isabelle too, and thanks them a dozen times.

"You do know you're impossible to buy for," Ava says.

Margaret beams. "This is just the perfect gift. And Saturday night—*primo marveloso!*" She really does look as happy—well, as happy as a kid on Christmas, even though she can go to any Broadway show on opening night and sit in the front row center.

"Who will you take with you?" Kelley asks.

Margaret shrugs. "Probably Drake, if he's still speaking to me."

"Drake?" Kelley says. He feels a pinch of jealousy. "Who's Drake?"

"Friend of mine," she says. "Pediatric brain surgeon at Sloan Kettering."

"Slacker," Kelley says.

Ava opens a sweater.

Kevin opens a subscription to *Sports Illustrated.*

Patrick opens another tie.

By the end of the morning, the pitcher of Golden Dreams is gone and the plate of muffins has been devoured. Ava plays some good, old-fashioned religious carols on the piano, and they all sing "O Holy Night," "We Three Kings," "The First Noel," "O Little Town of Bethlehem." Margaret has a rich alto that blends beautifully with Isabelle's clear soprano. Patrick is the strongest of the men. Together they sound pretty good, Kelley thinks. Or maybe he's just had one too many Golden Dreams.

"Play 'Silent Night,'" Kelley says.

"I will later," Ava says. "Right now, Mommy and I have to cook."

Margaret and Ava go back to the kitchen to prepare the standing rib roast, and Isabelle and Kevin snuggle up on the sofa. Patrick is subdued; he plops into the big armchair and starts reading the biography of Alexander Hamilton that Kelley got him. Patrick checks his phone every time he turns the page. Kelley is sure he's waiting for Jen to call. It's Christmas— she *will* call, right? No matter what Paddy has done, a man deserves to talk to his children on Christmas.

This gets Kelley thinking about Bart, which threatens his good mood. He sits in front of the fire. Bart has only been out of communication for six days, and what else would Kelley expect? He's fighting a *war* in *Afghanistan*. Still, Kelley worries. Bart is nineteen, a child still; he's only been shaving for four years and driving for two. He has done drugs and deflowered virgins and seen the band Kings of Leon something like fifteen times, but he is by no means worldly.

Where are you, Bart? Kelley wonders. *What are you doing?*

Thinking about Bart leads Kelley to thinking about Mitzi. What is *she* doing this Christmas? Does she miss Kelley? Miss the other kids? Miss the inn? Miss her nutcrackers? Miss her carolers? There are at least half a dozen presents for her under the tree from Kelley: the Eileen Fisher sweater she asked for, a platter shaped like a scallop shell, a pair of Alexis Bittar earrings, a gift certificate for a manicure and pedicure, and this year's ornament—a silver ring containing a needlepoint replica of the Winter Street Inn, exact down to the flower boxes and pineapple door knocker. None of the gifts are extravagant—he doesn't really have the money anymore to be extravagant—but they're thoughtful. He knows that all Mitzi really wants for Christmas is for Bart to be safe.

He decides, for several reasons, to call her—the most convincing reason is that it feels like the right thing to do. It's Christmas, and she's his wife.

My love feeds on your love, beloved.

He will never stop loving her. He thinks of Mitzi wearing a peach dress at his brother's funeral, Mitzi lying in the bath with her hair piled on top of her head, curled tendrils framing her face.

He dials her cell phone, figuring he'll end up leaving a

message—she's terrible when it comes to answering her cell phone—but she picks up on the first ring.

"Kelley?"

"Hi," he says, casually, almost cheerfully. "Merry Christmas."

"Oh," she says. "Thanks? Merry Christmas to you, too."

"Where are you?" he says. He realizes he never asked George yesterday where they were staying. He supposes he thought they might be sleeping in the back of the 1931 Model A fire engine.

"I'm at the Castle," she says.

"The Castle" is their name for the behemoth luxury hotel that summarily stole all of Winter Street's business. The building is opulent and beautifully appointed; it has a pool, a bar-restaurant, a spa, and a state-of-the-art fitness center. Kelley can't compete with that. People love amenities. Amenities trump home-baked muffins and four-poster beds any day of the week.

"You got a room at the Castle," Kelley says. He is close to hanging up. He might feel more betrayed about Mitzi's staying at the Castle than he does about George.

"It has no soul," Mitzi says. "Just like we always thought."

Of course it has no soul! Kelley thinks. He can't *believe* she is paying *money* to stay there. And he does *not* appreciate her use of the pronoun "we."

"Have you heard from Bart?" he asks. This is all he really needs to know.

"No," she says. "Have you?"

"No," he says.

They sit on the phone for a second in silence. He is terrified about the safety of his son; Mitzi must be a thousand times worse.

"Listen," he says, "would you and George like to come for Christmas dinner?"

Mitzi starts to cry. This comes as no surprise; she cries at AT&T long-distance commercials.

"I'd love to," she says. "Oh, thank you, Kelley! You have made my Christmas! What time should we come?"

"Come at five," Kelley says.

"We'll be there," she says.

AVA

As far as Christmases go, it isn't too bad. Her father has bought her cashmere sweaters from J.Crew in three colors, and her mother has gotten her a diamond circle necklace that is, without a doubt, the best gift of Christmas, and, furthermore, it is now the most beautiful and glamorous thing Ava owns. She wonders where she will ever wear it. It's too fancy to wear to work at Nantucket Elementary School, and when she and Nathaniel go out, they go to places like the Bar and the Faregrounds, neither of which is an appropriate place for a diamond circle necklace. If Nathaniel ever takes her back to the Wauwinet, she supposes she can wear it. And when she goes to visit Margaret in Manhattan.

Ava gently removes the necklace from the box and tries it on, looking in the hallway mirror.

She starts to cry.

Her mother is standing behind her in the mirror, and Ava can see how strongly they resemble each other, but even that doesn't cheer her.

Margaret says, "You don't like it?"

"I love it," Ava says, but her tears keep falling. What girl doesn't love diamonds? And yet it isn't the kind of diamond she wanted this Christmas. She wanted to be Isabelle—a girl whose boyfriend loves her so much, he surprised her with an engagement ring. The only person she identifies with is Patrick—his facial expression closely resembles her own. He has good reason: he has been abandoned by his wife and children. Ava's boyfriend has gone home for the holidays, which doesn't mean a thing—nobody has even asked where Nathaniel is—except to Ava. To Ava, it means she is unloved, unlovable, unwanted, undesirable.

Then she thinks about Scott Skyler, and her face grows warm. If Scott were here right now, she might let him kiss her again, maybe in her bedroom, lying on her bed with Scott on top of her.

Margaret says, "Now, there's a smile. That's what I like to see."

Ava waits until noon before she checks her phone. She only has a few moments, because her father wants her to play carols—("I will in a little while," Ava says, "but no 'Frosty,' no 'Silver Bells'...and absolutely no 'Jingle Bells.'")—and then she and Margaret must start making dinner.

She closes her bedroom door and takes a sustaining breath.

Nothing from Nathaniel. No missed calls, no texts. She even checks her e-mail, in case he lost his phone or dropped it in his wassail.

She plops down on the bed. She hates herself, hates the weak, groveling, infatuated-beyond-all-reason center of her being. Her core is made of Nathaniel jelly. She is 100 percent sure that if she asks Margaret, Margaret will say she has never been this far gone over a man before—not over Kelley, certainly. And any other boyfriend Margaret has ever had is eating his heart out right now.

She calls Nathaniel because she can't *not* call Nathaniel. He answers on the first ring. His voice is chipper, as if he has been awake for hours.

"Hey there," he says. "Merry Christmas."

"Merry Christmas to you," she says. She tries to match his jovial tone; he sounds like he's wishing the mailman a Merry Christmas. "Whatcha up to?"

"We're still opening presents, believe it or not," he says. "At least, I am. I just got home a little while ago."

"Home?" Ava says. "From where?"

"From the Cabots'," he says.

Cardiac arrest. Ava is going to die.

"You *slept* there?" she says.

"I passed out in the den," Nathaniel says. "Nobody even knew I was there until I popped up in the middle of their Christmas morning."

"Oh," Ava says. She has a hundred questions, among them: how did he end up in the den downstairs? He was down there drinking with Kirsten, it was safe to assume. "What, were you down there drinking with Kirsten until late?"

"It must have been late," Nathaniel says. "I'm not sure what time I zonked." He has a casual and open tone in delivering this news, as if nothing about it should give Ava pause.

"I called you at eleven o'clock," Ava says. "Your phone was off."

"Huh," he says. "That's weird. I mean, it wasn't *off*, but there's no reception in anyone's basement around here, so my phone probably just acted like it was off."

"Ah," Ava says. "Well, you said you'd call at nine, and you didn't."

"Yeah," he says. "I ended up hanging out."

Ava is silent, and so is Nathaniel. In the background, Ava can hear the high-pitched, happy screams of Nathaniel's nieces and nephews.

Finally, Nathaniel says, "Hey, so, how's Hawaii?"

"I didn't go," Ava says. "There's...a lot of stuff going on around here. So my mom just flew here instead."

"That's cool," Nathaniel says. "Your mom's there? Staying at the inn? How's Mitzi handling that?"

"Mitzi ran off," Ava says. "With George the Santa Claus."

Nathaniel laughs, not because he finds what she just said *completely absurd,* but, Ava thinks, because he suffers from selective listening and he's laughing in an attempt to humor her so he can get off the phone and enjoy his family.

"Wow," he says, confirming her suspicions. "Funny."

She says, "Well, I'll let you go."

"Hey!" he says, suddenly finding new energy. "Since you're home, you can open my present."

"Your present?" Ava says. Her heart resuscitates. "What present?"

"I dropped it off at the inn before I left on Tuesday," he says. "I gave it to Isabelle."

"You did?" Ava says. "That was thoughtful."

"Yeah," he says. "I wanted you to be able to open it."

"Thank you," Ava says.

"All right," he says. "Well, text me and let me know how you like it."

"I will," she says.

"I should go," he says. "Do you have plans for the rest of the day?"

"Dinner at five," Ava says. "Mom and I are cooking a standing rib roast."

"I can't believe your mom is there," Nathaniel says. "It probably seems normal to you because she's your mom, but to me it just seems really…I don't know…cool."

Ava crosses her eyes. She doesn't want to hear it.

"I'll talk to you later," she says.

"Oh, okay," Nathaniel says.

She pauses, waiting for him to say it first, but he never says it first.

"I love you," she says.

"Yep. Love you, too," he says, and they hang up.

Phone call: unsatisfactory, Ava thinks. If she lets herself dwell on what happened late last night in the "den," then it's *really* unsatisfactory. But her pain and angst are ameliorated by the anticipation of Nathaniel's present.

Ava marches out to the main room. Kevin and Isabelle are lounging on the sofa; Isabelle's eyes are closed. Kevin is stroking her hair.

"Is she asleep?" Ava whispers.

Kevin nods.

Crap. Ava sits on the ottoman, waiting for Isabelle to wake up so Ava can ask her where the present from Nathaniel is. There is nothing wrapped left under the tree except the gifts for Jennifer and Paddy's kids. Ava tries not to feel peeved that Isabelle never told her such a present existed; possibly Nathaniel asked Isabelle to keep it a secret.

What would a desirable present from Nathaniel be? Since he's not here to give it himself, Ava knows it's not a diamond ring. Any other jewelry would be good, especially earrings made by Jessica Hicks, who is Ava's favorite. Something Nathaniel made himself would be wonderful — a finely crafted wooden box with secret drawers where he might, someday soon, hide her diamond ring. Or a custom frame that holds a picture of the two of them — maybe the photo they took on her birthday that night at the Wauwinet. Ava has never looked happier in her life, she doesn't think, than on that night. Also acceptable would be concert tickets for a date in the spring or summer, something they could look forward to together; double points if it is Yo-Yo Ma or Charlotte Church or Beyoncé, all of whom are favorites of Ava's.

Isabelle's eyelids flutter open, and Ava pounces like a starving animal.

"Isabelle," she says. "Did Nathaniel drop off a present for me? Do you know where it is?"

Isabelle's eyes are unfocused. She blinks, rubs a hand across her lower abdomen, and Kevin tightens his grip. The sight of them *together* like *this* is still hard to process. For the past six months, Isabelle has been working at the inn like a French Cinderella. Ava has seen her cleaning rooms at seven in the morning and preparing for breakfast at nine at night. Ava did once happen across Kevin and Isabelle eating bowls of chocolate ice cream together in the kitchen in the middle of the afternoon, before Kevin left for his shift at the Bar, but Ava thought nothing of it.

Isabelle's voice is scratchy. "Yes," she says, and she smiles. "It is in the front closet. Nathaniel say surprise you."

The front closet! Ava thinks. She hops to her feet.

The front closet is used only for guests of the inn. It holds five matching umbrellas from the Nantucket Golf Club, a black coat someone must have left last night (or, possibly, the year before—Ava never opens the front closet, and she doubts anyone else does either), and Ava's present, wrapped in shiny red paper!

It's bigger than a bread box. Ava's heart thuds with worry; she remembers that good things come in small packages. She picks it up, a rectangular package, about two feet long and a foot wide. She shakes it; there is movement. She heads through the main room, toward the back of the house.

"Carols, Ava, please!" Kelley says. "We're all ready."

"In a minute," she says.

In the box from Nathaniel is a pair of dark-green Hunter rain boots with matching fleece socks. Ava holds a boot in her hand. Rubber rain boots. This is her Christmas gift.

"Ava!" her father calls.

Ava throws one boot across the room, then goes out to play the carols.

PATRICK

One thirty, eastern standard time, ten thirty on the West Coast. Jen and the kids will be finished opening presents but not yet headed to the Park Tavern. He should call, despite his shame. She must be thinking he isn't at all the man she married.

Just then, a call comes in from the disposable cell phone of Bucky Larimer. Patrick wants to throw his phone into the fire, but instead he stands, opens the front door, and steps out into the cold day to take the call.

"What?" he says.

"Man, thank *God* you finally answered," Bucky says.

"What," Patrick says, "do you want?" There is a way in which he can see this *whole thing* as Bucky's fault; certainly the plan was created at Bucky's instigation: he was the one who pulled Patrick aside and said he had a handle on a sure thing and asked if there was any way Patrick could help him capitalize on it. Patrick is guilty of being too weak to resist—and then, of course, of taking the poor decision to the $25-million level.

Bucky says, "I confessed."

"What?" Patrick says.

"I turned myself in."

"And you turned me in," Patrick says.

"Well," Bucky says, "by default, yes."

"What exactly did you say?" Patrick asks.

"I told them what happened," Bucky says.

"Who is 'they?' " Patrick asks.

"The feds."

"You named me."

"Man, I had no choice."

"What *exactly* did you say?"

"That I told you about MDP, told you it was headed for FDA approval, and you asked me if I wanted to invest some money on my behalf in exchange for the information."

"Whoa!" Patrick says. "Wait a minute! That is NOT how it happened."

"What isn't?"

"*You* asked *me* if I would invest for you in exchange for the info."

"No," Bucky says. "It was the other way around."

"It was NOT!" Patrick shouts, and his voice is so loud that every house on Winter Street seems to shimmy on its foundation.

"Anyway," Bucky says, "I just wanted to let you know what was up."

"What's *up*," Patrick says, "is that I am headed to *jail* because of *you!* And I have a *wife!* And three kids!"

"I know, man," Bucky says. But Bucky *doesn't* know. Bucky doesn't have so much as a steady girlfriend. At the reunion, he was hitting on the hot women from their graduating class, all of whom were married. That alone proves the man has no scruples.

"Answer me this," Patrick says. He has gone outside without a coat, and he's freezing.

"What?"

"Are you going to jail? Or are they taking it easy on you because you sold me out?"

"Well," Bucky says.

That's all Patrick needs to hear. He hangs up the phone.

He screams an expletive at the quiet Nantucket street. Luckily, he thinks, Winter Street is only three houses long, and the other owners are summer people.

He calls Jen. What does he have to lose now? His life is over. He will lose his job and go to jail, and he will be lucky if he goes to jail for insider trading and not first-degree murder, because he seriously wants to KILL Bucky Larimer.

Please, he thinks. *Please, Jennifer, answer the phone.*

He gets her voice mail almost immediately. He wants to throw his phone down the street, but instead he leaves a message.

"Baby, it's me." He swallows. "I'm in big trouble, bigger than maybe we thought on Tuesday. I'm on Nantucket, at the inn; I'm drowning here without you. Call me, please. I need to hear your voice. I need to talk to the boys." He swallows. "I've been having some pretty dark thoughts...anyway, please call me."

"Patrick?"

Patrick hangs up the phone and turns around. His mother is standing in the doorway.

"Are you okay, honey?" she asks.

Patrick hasn't talked to his mother about any of this because he didn't want to ruin her Christmas. He was happy to see her, but having her here also puts a finer point on his shame.

He shakes his head no. She closes the door behind her and comes down the front walk toward him, even though she's only wearing sweats she borrowed from Ava and a pair of Kelley's Irish-knit socks.

"I messed up, Mom," he says.

She puts her arms around him. "Your father told me, sweetheart."

He starts to cry. He has cried more in the past two days than he has in the rest of his life combined. "I really messed up. And Jen is gone. She won't answer my calls, and I don't blame her. It's going to be in the newspapers. It's going to publicly humiliate her and the kids...and you."

"Oh, honey," Margaret says. "Please don't worry about me. I'm a grown-up. I can handle it."

"I'm sorry, Mom," Patrick says. "I let you down, I let everybody down. One idiotic decision, and the whole house of cards falls."

"I've seen it again and again and again," Margaret says. "John Edwards, Tiger Woods, Eliot Spitzer, Lance Armstrong, A-Rod, Mark Sanford, Arnold Schwarzenegger—the list goes on and on. People are fallible, Patrick. People make bad decisions every second of every day. Do you want my advice?"

"Yes," Patrick says. He expected advice from his father

the night before, but, although his father was empathetic, he offered little in the way of practical help.

"Hold your head up high, admit what you did wrong, apologize, and accept your punishment."

He nods. "Okay."

"I have the name of a very good lawyer," she says. "The best. And he owes me a favor."

"Okay," Patrick says.

Margaret hugs him again. "I know it feels pretty awful right now. But your father and I know you're not a bad person. We love you unconditionally."

"Okay," he says.

"Do you know what 'unconditionally' means?"

He nods, but he wants to hear it anyway.

Margaret says, "It means *no matter what*."

KEVIN

Margaret and Patrick are out in the front yard, and Ava is in her bedroom, so it's the perfect time to ask.

"Dad?" Kevin says. "Since Isabelle is pregnant and everything, we were wondering…"

Kelley leans forward, his hands tented. He says, "Yes?"

"We were wondering if..." Kevin can't quite figure out how to say what he wants to say, despite having rehearsed it.

"If we can take over running the inn," Isabelle says.

Kelley laughs. "Where were you twelve years ago?"

Kevin isn't quite sure how to respond to that. Twelve years ago, he was still married to Norah, living in their cottage, working at the Bar.

"Isabelle already knows how to run the inn," Kevin says. "And I can learn."

"I'm selling the inn," Kelley says.

KELLEY

He actually forgets about his conversation with Eddie Pancik the night before until Kevin and Isabelle ask if they can take over the running of the inn.

"I'm selling the inn," Kelley says, and for the first time ever, it isn't just an idle threat. As soon as Eddie Pancik and his wife, Grace, walked into the party, Eddie was upon Kelley. First he gave Kelley a dozen organic eggs, which was not an insubstantial gift. Mitzi insisted on buying eggs from Grace Pancik, and they sold for eleven dollars a dozen, another reason Kelley is going broke. Kelley then thought to broach the topic of selling the inn with Eddie, but, as it turned out, Eddie had seen Kelley's Facebook post. *FSBO. $4M.*

He really *is* Fast Eddie.

Eddie said, "Are you serious about selling this place? Because I know someone who would be interested."

"As an inn?" Kelley said.

"No," Eddie said, "as a private home."

This felt a little funny to Kelley. The house was built in 1873 by a grocer, but it had been operated as an inn since the turn of the century. Kelley and Mitzi had always honored this history. Even as they did their renovation, they were determined to preserve all the interior historical elements. If Eddie Pancik sold it as a private home, walls would be knocked down and cathedral ceilings installed; it would become one more showstopper of white bead board and custom-painted floors.

But—Kelley is too broke to be a preservationist.

"Call me on Friday," Kelley said to Eddie Pancik. "I'm serious. I'd like to sell it as soon as humanly possible."

Kevin and Isabelle appear thunderstruck at Kelley's pronouncement.

"Where are you…we all…going to live, then?" Kevin says. "If you sell it?"

"*When* I sell it," Kelley says. "It's happening. Someone is already interested." The kids are looking at him like he just gobbled down the last potato before the famine, and it dawns on him that he's basically just evicted Kevin and fired

Isabelle—and on Christmas Day, no less! When they are so happy about their own news!

"We'll buy something else," Kelley says. "Something smaller for me, and maybe I can help get you kids set up with something of your own." He throws the "maybe" and the "help" in there to emphasize the conditional nature of his offer. Because, although he feels guilty about dismantling their lives in one fell swoop, Kevin is thirty-six years old and still living at home. Isabelle is a smart cookie; once she marries Kevin and gets her green card, the sky is the limit. It's a tough stance for a parent, but what the two of them may need is a kick in the ass, right out the door of this inn, so that they are given sufficient impetus to go out and improve their lives.

Still, the expressions on their faces are difficult to ignore.

"It will be fine," Kelley says, hoping this is true. "Everything will be just fine." And with that, he heads back to his bedroom and his computer so he can e-mail Bart.

MARGARET

After she and Ava stick the standing rib roast in the oven and trim the asparagus and wash the spinach, Margaret checks her phone.

She has one text, from Drake.

It says: *I can't believe how much I miss you. Will you marry me?*

She laughs! Proposed to, at the age of fifty-nine, by text message! My, how the times have changed.

Probably because she is with Kelley now, floating in some kind of nostalgic bubble with him, she instantly remembers when Kelley proposed.

New York City, May 18, a year in the last millennium. Kelley was about to graduate from Columbia Business School, but Margaret had one more semester at NYU before she got her master's in communications. They were *so poor*—when they had been dating for six months, Margaret gave up her room in the NYU dorms to save money and she moved in with Kelley uptown. They cooked pasta during the week and treated themselves to pizza and a movie on Friday nights and Chinese delivery on Sundays. Margaret got the occasional job doing voice-overs for WQXR, and when those checks came in, she and Kelley blew them on shows at CBGB or something fancier, like dinner at Tavern on the Green or drinks at the bar at Beekman Tower.

On May 18, however, Kelley had just gotten a job offer from Prudential Securities, a job that paid nearly six figures a year—but Margaret didn't know this yet. On May 18, Margaret was at jury duty, a fate worse than death, because that week in May was absurdly, unseasonably hot, and the air-conditioning in the courthouse was on the blink, and Margaret didn't have *time* for jury duty! She had papers and exams, and she was trying to get an internship at the local CBS affiliate.

On May 18, Margaret emerged from the courthouse sweating and irate and dreading the interminable subway ride from the bottom of Manhattan to the top.

There was a man dressed in a black suit and white shirt on the steps of the courthouse, holding a placard with her name on it: *Margaret Pryor.*

Margaret was confused. He looked like one of the chauffeurs who pick up fancy people at the airport.

Margaret said, "Are you looking for me?"

"Yes, miss," he said. "Follow me."

Margaret didn't *want* to follow a strange man. For all she knew, this was an abduction. Margaret had a friend at NYU, Leo, who was somehow related to John Gotti.

Mob, Margaret thought. Or possibly something worse? Possibly one or both of her parents had died, and her wealthy aunt Susan had sent this driver?

She tentatively followed the man in the black suit to a white stretch limousine waiting on the street.

Mob.

The back door opened from the inside, and Margaret felt a luscious blast of real air-conditioning.

She poked her head in and gasped. Kelley sat in the back, wearing his ripped khaki shorts and a Meat Loaf T-shirt. He had a bottle of champagne on ice and a dozen roses wrapped in cellophane.

"What...?" Margaret said.

"I got the job!" he said.

Margaret climbed into the limousine, kissed Kelley, and congratulated him profusely. Then she began sucking on an ice cube.

"I can't believe you got a limo!" she said.

Kelley popped the champagne. "I only got it to drive us home," he said. "So we'd better drink this fast."

But as it turned out, they had one stop to make before they reached their squalid apartment uptown. The driver pulled up in front of the Metropolitan Museum of Art, which was where Margaret and Kelley had first met.

"Oh," Margaret said. She didn't want to be a spoilsport, but she wasn't in the mood for the Miró exhibit or the Temple of Dendur.

Kelley pulled a box out of the pocket of his disintegrating shorts and presented her with a small but sparkling diamond.

"Marry me," Kelley said. "Please, please, Margaret, marry me."

Margaret smiles at the memory. Their kids call it the Quarter-Pounder Proposal, because it's heavy on the *cheese*. Proposed to in a white stretch limo by a guy wearing a Meat Loaf T-shirt, offering roses he bought at the Korean deli? But what Margaret has never been able to explain to their kids is how sweet and earnest Kelley was on that day. She and Kelley were young, they were poor—but with their prospects improving—and they were in love. The air-conditioning had felt so delicious, the ice on her tongue, divine.

Kelley could teach Drake a thing or two, Margaret thinks.

AVA

As she and Margaret prepare the standing rib roast and the rest of the meal, Ava tells her mother about the gift of Hunter boots with matching socks.

"Matching socks?" Margaret says. "Maybe I'll get a pair. Do you remember how when it snows in the city, the slush puddles up, and you step off the street corner and almost drown?"

"You can have mine," Ava says. She sighs. "Nathaniel doesn't love me."

"It's not the most romantic gift," Margaret says.

Then Ava tells her mother about kissing Scott in the kitchen. Ava has been thinking about the kissing more than she thought she would. She finds herself checking the clock, wishing for time to move more quickly so that Scott will get here. She wonders if Scott will be brave enough to kiss her again; she worries he won't be. If she wants to kiss him, she might have to instigate it.

But she doesn't tell her mother this. What she says is: *I was pretty drunk last night, and I let Scott Skyler kiss me.*

Margaret says, "Scott Skyler, your assistant principal?"

Ava nods.

Margaret chops the woody ends off the asparagus. "I never did have an affair with any of my bosses," she says. "I've always felt proud of that."

Ava says, "I'm pretty confused."

Margaret says, "I'm not a relationship expert. Clearly. But I've dated a lot of men since your father and I split, and, in my experience, the more you push a man away, the more fervently he comes after you. If I were in your shoes, I would call Nathaniel and tell him it's over."

Ava would no sooner break up with Nathaniel than she would set her piano on fire.

But then, as she and Margaret cut the stems off the fresh spinach and crisp the bacon for the hot bacon dressing, and as Margaret makes cranberry-thyme butter for the snowflake rolls (she did a segment on *The Chew* with Rachael Ray, and look what she learned!), Ava thinks to herself, *What if I did?*

He passed out in Kirsten's den? He didn't call because *he decided to hang out?* He gave her *rubber rain boots* for Christmas? If Ava stays with Nathaniel, things will never improve. It will always be her chasing him. Does she want that?

No, she does not.

*   *   *

When she and her mother are finished in the kitchen, Ava goes into the bedroom to call Nathaniel.

He answers on the first ring. "Looking good, Billy Ray," he says sleepily. She must have woken him up from a nap. He's tired because he barely slept the night before. Still, Ava is temporarily derailed by the vision of Nathaniel entangled in the covers of his childhood bed, and so she plays along.

"Feeling good, Louis," she says.

"Whatcha doin'?" he asks. "Did you have a nice Christmas? Did you like your present?"

"The boots?" she says. "Very practical, thank you."

"You always wear little ballet shoes, even in the rain and snow," he says. "And I worry about you. I don't want you to get sick. I need you around."

She says, "Yeah, well, about that."

"About what?" he says.

"About needing me around." Ava takes a deep breath. "Listen, this isn't working out for me."

"What isn't?" he says. "Are you mad because I came *home?*"

"This relationship," Ava says. "You and me, me and you, us together—it isn't making me happy."

"Because I came home. Because you think I came back to see Kirsten, which I did *not*. I mean, she's an old friend, and she's at a low point, but I can't help her, and I'm certainly not going to rekindle any kind of romance with her. That was over *long* ago, and over is over, especially in this case."

Ava's heart relaxes at those words, and she nearly abandons ship. Nathaniel hasn't talked this frankly to her about his emotional state, ever. But Ava is on a mission here, and once she's on a mission, she won't be derailed.

"This isn't about you and Kirsten," Ava says. "This is about you and me. I need more—more love, more affection, more intimacy, more of a sense that we have a future."

"What do you mean by 'future'?" Nathaniel asks. "Do you mean you want to get *married?*"

He makes it sound preposterous, as though marriage were the equivalent of running the Boston Marathon backward or enrolling in clown school.

"That's how the human race has made it this far," Ava says. "They marry and they procreate."

Silence on Nathaniel's end. She has scared him to death. She is right to proceed. Instead of feeling like all her blood is pooling at her feet, she feels empowered. She's wasted nearly two years of her precious twenties swimming in a pool of unrequited love.

She says, "Scott Skyler has been around a lot the past couple days. Last night he wore the Santa suit, since George stole Mitzi away from my dad."

"So...what?" Nathaniel says. "This isn't about Kirsten, after all? This is about *Scott?* I'm well aware, Ava, that Scott is crazy about you. But I thought you were immune to that."

Ava considers telling Nathaniel about kissing Scott, but that seems cruel. She says, "I want to be treated like *someone precious*. I want to be someone's *beloved*. I never feel that way with you, and it dawned on me at some point today that I'm never *going* to feel that way with you, ever."

"Ava," Nathaniel says, and it sounds like he's pleading. She figures this is a good way to leave it.

"Good-bye, Nathaniel," she says, and she hangs up.

MARGARET

She bumps into Kelley in the hallway of the back house. It's still very strange, wandering around the inn—and especially the owners' quarters—like this, since it has always been verboten by Mitzi.

"I should probably shower before we eat dinner," she says. "Which bathroom should I use?"

"Use mine," he says.

Margaret thinks he might proposition her again—and she would be a willing accomplice—but Kelley looks morose.

"What's wrong?" she says. "Are the Golden Dreams wearing off?"

"I just e-mailed Bart," Kelley says. "Wished him a Merry

Christmas. He hasn't answered my last two e-mails or the past three texts. Do you have any idea how unnerving that is?"

"No," she says. "I have no idea. None of our children went to war. I'm sure it's perfectly awful."

"Awful," Kelley says. "There have been double-digit deaths over there this week. I purposely haven't checked the news today because it's Christmas, and I just…can't."

Margaret gnaws on her lower lip. If ever there were a time to tell Kelley about the missing convoy, it's now. But the number-one ironclad rule of broadcast journalism is to make sure your news is true. She's fairly certain a convoy holding forty-five soldiers has been overtaken by insurgent nationals, but whether or not Bartholomew Quinn was on that convoy, she can't possibly say. Giving partial information to Kelley at this point will cause him anxiety of unknown proportions and will ruin his Christmas.

And yet, Margaret feels like she's lying.

"We have a saying at CBS," she says. "No news is bad news—but that's strictly a network perspective. In your case, no news is good news."

"I worry," Kelley says. "These god-awful scenarios go through my head."

"You're his father," Margaret says.

"He's so young," Kelley says.

"I'm praying for him," Margaret says. "And I will continue to pray for him until he's safely home."

"Thank you," Kelley says. "I'm happy to hear that Margaret Quinn still prays."

"All the time," Margaret says. She reaches out and squeezes his arm. "Well, I'm off for the shower."

"Is it wildly inappropriate to admit that I'd really like to join you?" Kelley says.

"Borderline inappropriate," she confirms. But she's not surprised. The opposite of death, she supposes, is sex.

"So is that a no?" Kelley asks.

"Bring your own towel," Margaret says. "I still don't like to share."

PATRICK

Kevin says, "Have you seen Mom and Dad?"

"No," Patrick says. He's pretending to read, but really he's staring at the face of his phone, trying to send one of the most difficult texts of his life.

"It's so weird to even say their names together like that," Kevin says. "And I know this is going to sound nuts, but I think there's something going on between them."

"Confirmed," Patrick says. "I saw the two of them sneaking out of Dad's bedroom. They had definitely been going at it."

Ava plops down on the sofa next to Kevin and Isabelle. "How are we supposed to feel about that? Our divorced parents are having a fling. Does anyone have the manual for How to Deal with Completely Screwed-Up Family Situations?"

"I would choose to be happy for them," Isabelle says.

"I'm happy for them," Kevin says.

Ava sighs. "I broke up with Nathaniel."

"You did not," Kevin says.

"I did," she says. "Just now, over the phone."

"Was it the boots?" Kevin asks. "Because I'm clueless, but even I know that boots are a sucky present."

"The boots are symptomatic of a bigger problem," Ava says. "I am not Nathaniel Oscar's great, passionate love. I'm just not."

Patrick stands up. He doesn't want them to think he's a heartless bastard, but he has actual problems. Forget that he has committed an egregious white-collar crime for a second. He didn't just break up with his boyfriend/girlfriend. His wife of fourteen years walked out on him, taking his three sons away from him on Christmas. He can't get any of them on the phone. He called Jen's mother's *house* and nobody answered. He, for one, is thrilled his parents are getting it on, because at this point it looks like Jennifer will ask him for a divorce, and Patrick's only glimmer of hope is that twenty years from now, he and Jen will reunite in a similar manner.

As Patrick heads back to the owners' quarters, there's a knock at the door, and Patrick whips around. It's Scott, the assistant principal. He's wearing jeans, a tweedy jacket, and a red Vineyard Vines tie printed with bluefish wearing Santa hats. It's the very same tie Jennifer bought Patrick to wear to the Everlast Christmas party.

Every part of Patrick's body hurts.

Ava jumps up from the sofa to greet Scott.

Well, Patrick thinks, *Nathaniel was easily replaced.* And once Patrick goes to jail, he supposes he will be replaced as well.

Jennifer and the boys. How is he supposed to live without them?

Patrick locks himself in Bart's room; Lindsay Lohan stares him down. He composes a text to Gary Grimstead: *I won't ruin your holiday, but a full confession will be forthcoming tomorrow. You have my most humble apology, man. I got tripped up. But I will do everything in my power not to take you down with me. Peace, PQ*

He hits Send. It goes. It's done. He will lose his job, accept his lashings from the press; he will go to jail and serve his time.

He feels a big, fat bong hit is in order. He fills Bart's purple glass bong with fresh water and packs in some weed from the bag in Bart's top drawer. It's been a long time since he's done this (not really: just since that trip to South Beach with the Playboy models, none of whom he so much as talked to, by the way).

He holds the smoke for as long as he can, then releases it.

Ahhhhhhhh. His mind-set realigns almost immediately. Leave it to Bart to have some really choice drugs.

Patrick walks back out to the main room, thinking he will stare at the tree until he falls asleep; his mother will awaken him when dinner is ready. The aroma of the meat roasting is *insane!*

There's a knock at the front door—another knock? Patrick tightens the belt of his bathrobe. It's probably not a bad idea to pursue getting dressed at some point, especially since soon enough he will be wearing an orange jumpsuit. This thought strikes him as hilarious, and he starts giggling.

Ava opens the front door and—Ava screams. Happy? Sad? Scared? Patrick can't tell.

Happy!

Jen and the kids walk in.

Whaaaaaaaaat? Patrick slaps himself in the face: *Wake up, wake up!* But it's real; they're here! Pierce wraps his arms around Auntie Ava, the two of them being favorite friends, and Jen ushers in Barrett and Jaime. Jaime comes barreling toward Patrick—Jaime the baby, the little guy. Patrick scoops him up.

"Daddy!"

He's Daddy once again—oh, thank God! Tears start building up behind his eyes, but he can't cry in front of his children. He is big, strong Daddy—Daddy, Master of the Universe. He *cannot* cry, but, wow—man, is he grateful.

Ava is good, she is brilliant; Patrick will never say a negative word about her again, because she herds the kids over to the Christmas tree, saying, "Guess what, guys, Santa stopped here for you!" This gives Patrick a moment of reunion with his wife.

"Jen...," he says.

She slips quietly into his arms, right where she belongs. Haven't they always marveled at how perfectly they fit together?

She buries her face inside his bathrobe. "Have you been *smoking?*" she asks.

"Yes," he says. "I did a bong hit in Bart's room. I was feeling...pretty low."

"God," she says, "I want a bong hit. Later, though, when the boys are asleep."

He squeezes her tighter. They are always on the same page. "I missed you so much," he says. "I nearly died from missing you."

"We didn't go to California," she says. "I got as far as the Hilton at Logan. We spent a couple nights there, which the kids hated. So this morning we went back home and opened presents, and I ate the rest of the caviar, since it was open..."

The caviar, he thinks. He has so many things to be sorry about.

"Then, in the bathroom, I saw the bottle of Vicodin. I'm so glad you didn't do anything stupid."

"I did do something stupid," he says.

She puts a finger across his lips, and then she kisses him. "Let's talk about it later," she says. "Right now, I'm just happy to be with you."

Patrick wants to throw her over his shoulder and carry her back to Bart's room to show her how happy *he* is. But at that moment, Kelley and Margaret emerge from the owners' quarters, both of them freshly showered.

"Grandchildren!" Margaret cries with unmitigated glee.

"Your mother?" Jen asks. She runs a hand through her short, dark hair, and Patrick knows she is wishing for lipstick.

"Long story," Patrick says.

"Where's Mitzi?" Jen asks.

But he'll have to explain later, because the room is suddenly a three-ring circus, with kids laughing and wrapping paper flying in the air and Kelley saying, "I didn't think this day could *get* any better."

Patrick marvels at how one of the best feelings in the world is finding something precious that he thought was gone forever.

KELLEY

We're all on the same page, right? No one is to treat Mitzi any differently than they ever have. There is to be no judgment. Everything happens for a reason.

Kelley doesn't want to get into the particulars, but, suffice it to say, he isn't blameless in this.

Yes, Dad, fine, Dad, gotcha. We know, Dad.

Kelley looks pointedly at Isabelle. Ironically, she's the one he worries about the most.

"We're on the same page, right?" he says.

"Right," Isabelle says.

Margaret holds her palms up. "Don't look at me," she says. "I *like* Mitzi."

"Liar," Kelley says.

"I do!" Margaret insists.

Mitzi and George arrive at five o'clock on the dot. They both look uncomfortable, bordering on nauseated. George is wearing a lavender argyle sweater that seems like it might have been a Christmas gift from someone—Mitzi?—who hopes George loses thirty pounds in the near future; the cashmere strains over George's belly and barely meets the top of his pants. Mitzi is wearing a sage-green velvet dress (an Eileen Fisher, Kelley knows, that retails for $375) and a jaunty red suede fedora.

A hat! On Mitzi! A hat George must have made and Mitzi must have gamely agreed to wear to Christmas dinner hosted by the man she has been betraying for twelve years.

"Nice hat!" Kelley says. He kisses Mitzi on the cheek. "Merry Christmas. I'm glad you came."

"Thank you for having us," George says. He hands Kelley a gift bag containing a bottle of Johnnie Walker Black.

"Thank *you*, kind sir!" Kelley says. He hands the bottle off to Kevin, who whisks it to the bar.

Mitzi hands Kelley a present. It's a book; he knows which one. He'll save it to open at the dinner table, in case there's an awkward silence.

Patrick and Jen greet Mitzi, Ava says Merry Christmas, then Scott and Isabelle say Merry Christmas and *Joyeux Noël,* then Kevin offers drinks. Everyone puts in an order for something stronger than normal.

Mitzi says, "Do you have any white wine, Kevin?"

Kevin raises his eyebrows. "Wine?"

Kelley says, "You've been gone two days, and suddenly you drink wine?"

"It's Christmas," Mitzi says. "I sometimes drink wine on Christmas."

"You *never* drank wine on Christmas," Kelley says. "You never drank wine, ever. Unless, of course, you drank it in George's room?"

George says, "If you have white wine, Kevin, Mitzi would like a glass."

Oh, George, so gallant, making Kelley look like he's picking a fight.

Mitzi says, "Have you heard from Bart?"

"I have not," Kelley says. "Have you?"

"No," she says.

As far as Kelley is concerned, they have nothing else to say to each other. Wow—he is angrier than he thought he'd be.

George says to Scott, "How'd it go as Santa Claus?"

"Great," Scott says, grinning.

"Scott was a natural," Kelley says. "I hate to tell you this, George, but you've been replaced. Happens to the best of us."

"Daddy," Ava says.

Right, Kelley knows. He gives everyone else a lecture about being pleasant, and he alone is acting abominable.

At that moment, Margaret pops out of the kitchen wearing Mitzi's Christmas apron, featuring a silk-screened Rudolph with a red sequin nose. "Merry Christmas, everyone!" she sings out.

Kelley has no need for further jabs, because he has just unveiled his secret weapon. The look on Mitzi's face is *PRICELESS.* There is horror and jealousy wrapped up in complete shock.

Kelley would dance a jig if it were not so indelicate.

Mitzi turns to Kelley with icy-hot eyes, then back to Margaret. "Hello, Margaret."

"Hello, Mitzi," Margaret says. She sails over and embraces Mitzi warmly. The woman has the grace of a queen, Kelley thinks. "Merry Christmas. Today must be bittersweet for you, with Bart away. Please know I'm keeping him in my prayers."

"Oh," Mitzi says. "Thank you. Yes, it's been...difficult. Christmas morning at a hotel, everything topsy-turvy."

Well, whose fault is *that?* Kelley thinks.

Kevin arrives with Mitzi's wine and a whiskey, rocks, for both George and Kelley. Margaret, Ava, and Jennifer are drinking champagne. Patrick, Kevin, and Scott have vodka martinis. Isabelle has seltzer.

"I'd like to make a toast," Kelley says. "To all the members of the Quinn family who are present, and to the newest addition."

"Hear, hear," Kevin says, and he kisses Isabelle.

"What addition?" Mitzi says.

But nobody answers.

They are seated for dinner. Kelley takes his usual place and Margaret sits at Kelley's right, which is where Mitzi used to sit. Next to Margaret are Patrick, the three boys, Jennifer, Scott, Ava, George, Mitzi, Kevin, and Isabelle, who is next to Kelley.

Isabelle says to Mitzi, "*Ton chapeau.* Your hat." She makes a motion indicating Mitzi should take it off.

Mitzi looks flustered and embarrassed, and Kelley's heart

goes out to her. She never wears hats and hence is unaware that hats are inappropriate at the dinner table.

Kevin pours a nice pinot noir for everyone at the table who is drinking, which again seems to include Mitzi.

"Something smells delicious," George says.

"Standing rib roast," Margaret says. "That's what we used to have when the kids were growing up."

"And Yorkshire pudding made with the drippings," Ava says.

Again, the look on Mitzi's face is priceless. She may be drinking wine, but Kelley will bet a pretty penny she won't eat beef or anything made with "drippings." Just the word "drippings" is probably enough to send Mitzi to the hospital for a month.

Everything about the present situation delights him.

When everyone is seated, he reaches out, encouraging them to hold hands for the blessing.

He says, "O Lord, we thank you for the meal before us, lovingly prepared" — pause, let Mitzi consider — "and we are grateful for all of the family and friends assembled at this table. We also remember, O Lord, the ones who are *not* at this table tonight, especially our beloved Bart, who is overseas, defending our freedom. Please, Lord, keep Bart safe from bodily harm and let him know he is in our thoughts and prayers. Let us take a moment of silence to pray for Bart."

Silence.

MARGARET

She's squeezing Kelley's fingers so hard, she's surprised his fingers don't break. *Please let Bart be okay! Not on that convoy!* Her most recent memory of Bart is from eighteen months previous, when Bart's senior class came to New York City. Margaret offered the class a guided tour of CBS studios, with herself, "Bart's stepmother," as their guide. Bart texted her before the class arrived, saying, "I told everyone you were my stepmom, okay? Hashtag *avoidconfusion.*"

Margaret laughed and laughed at this. She is something of a reverse stepmother to Bart, the first wife of his father, the mother to his half siblings. Why isn't there a term for this relationship? Surely, there must be thousands of instances. Maybe because an actual relationship between a woman and the child of her ex-husband is so rare?

Margaret has always been fond of Bart. He has characteristics of Kelley's that her own kids do not—Kelley's aquiline nose, his golden hair, his sense of mischief. Bart got in a lot of trouble growing up. But then, so did Kelley.

The day Bart came into the studio, Margaret was as motherly as possible; she kissed him hello, she tousled his shaggy hair (all shaved off now, she supposes), she teased him about his excellent grades, or lack thereof. He had glowed from all her attentions, and at the end he hugged her and said, "Thanks, Mmmmmm." She hadn't been sure if he meant to call her Margaret or Mom.

"For you," she said. "Anything, anytime, always and forever."

His grin, both sweet and wicked, was *all Kelley.*

She misses him, she who honestly barely knows him. How must everyone else feel?

AVA

Ava is chastened. She has been so busy fretting about her relationship with Nathaniel that she hasn't had two seconds left over to think about Bart.

She and Bart used to be...*so close.* When he was born, Ava was ten years old; she would push him in his stroller, pretending he was *her* baby. He had soft, chubby cheeks and blue eyes and blond chick fuzz on top of his head. He was a living doll.

When Ava was a teenager, the thrill of taking care of Bart wore off a little. She was *always* called on to babysit him, and when she turned sixteen and got her license, she was enlisted to drive him and his pesky friends all over the island. Did she complain?

Yes, she complained. She called him a spoiled brat. Mitzi

never punished him, he was never held accountable for his actions, and as he grew older, his actions became more and more atrocious. He started smoking at fourteen. Ava caught him and his friend Michael, each with a cigarette, in the back parking lot of the high school. She turned him in to Mitzi, who cried and blamed herself. Bart hosted enormous parties at Dionis Beach with beer he stole out the back door of the Bar. He crashed three cars in eighteen months, he got caught repeatedly with marijuana—by Kelley and Mitzi, by the high school principal, by the police—and he broke and entered a summer house in Pocomo one weekend night in February when he and his derelict friends were bored.

But Ava doesn't want to spend her moment of silence running down Bart's rap sheet. What a person does isn't the same as who a person is. Bart is charming, fun loving, mischievous, and magnetic. Bart is her little brother, and Ava needs him to be safe.

ISABELLE

Dear Lord, please keep Bart in the palm of your hand. In the name of the Father, and of the Son, and of the Holy Spirit. Amen.

KEVIN

He has been having a great Christmas, the best of his life, perhaps. He remembers Eric Metz giving away money he could most certainly use. *This is for Nantucket Hospice,* Eric said. *They made things so much easier for my mom at the end.*

Grace, Kevin reminds himself.

He prays for Bart—*Bart, man, stay well, stay safe, stay strong, be smart, not reckless, don't take any unnecessary risks, Mitzi needs you, man, and so does Dad.*

Kevin has been convinced that Bart wears a Teflon shield, that everything slides off him, but right now, Kevin becomes aware that, wherever Bart is, he is probably scared and more than a little lonely.

We're thinking of you, man.

PATRICK

Patrick has spent the past nineteen years being a mentor and a role model for Bart, but no longer. Now, the tables have turned—Patrick is the screwup and Bart is the hero, and who would have ever predicted that?

Before Bart left for Germany, he spent the night with Patrick, Jen, and the kids in Boston. Jen made roast chicken and potatoes and a banana cream pie, because it's Bart's favorite. After dinner and tucking in the kids, Patrick and Bart walked over to Silvertone and had a couple of drinks. Patrick told the bartender, Murph, that Bart was shipping overseas with the Marines, and with that, the fact that Bart was nineteen was ignored, and the first round was on the house.

Patrick said, "So, are you nervous?"

"God, no," Bart said. "I'm pumped."

"It'll be good for you to get off the island," Patrick said.

"Yeah," Bart said. "I think Mom and Dad have finally run out of patience with me. And I don't want to go to college, not right now, anyway. I'd party my ass off, flunk out, come home to Nantucket, and work as the first mate on some fishing boat the rest of my life. The Marines, man, it *means* something. Defending our country, our freedom, so people like you can go out and make millions of dollars each day."

Patrick had laughed. They had done a shot of Jameson together with Murph, they had played some Kings of Leon on the jukebox, they had arm wrestled, and Bart had won. They had stumbled home arm in arm. Patrick experienced brotherly feelings he'd never had with Kevin, probably because he and Kevin were so close in age, raised as twins, or as two halves of the same person—the go-getter and the slacker, the perfectionist and the one who liked to half-ass things. Bart looked up to Patrick instead of resenting him, as Kevin did, and that felt good.

Patrick sighs. He thinks, *Be honorable, wherever you are, Bart. Do the right thing instead of the easy thing.*

KELLEY

Amen," he says, and he squeezes hands with Margaret and Isabelle.

Margaret and Ava serve dinner: the standing rib roast, the Yorkshire pudding, roasted asparagus, spinach salad with fresh mushrooms, cherry tomatoes, and hot bacon dressing, snowflake rolls with cranberry butter.

Mitzi, Kelley notices, takes only asparagus and a roll — and then, on second thought, another roll and a small serving of salad.

Kelley wants to introduce a nostalgic topic of conversation, and the first thing that pops into his mind is the genesis of this family. The way he met Margaret. The kids all know this story — he used to tell it every Christmas — but Isabelle hasn't heard it, and neither has Scott or George; nor have the grandchildren.

"My first Christmas in Manhattan," Kelley says, "I was so *poor*."

"Oh boy," Ava says. She slugs back some wine, then feeds him the next line. "How poor were you, Daddy?"

"Well, I was putting myself through business school at Columbia and living in a university-owned apartment with four roommates."

"And one disgusting bathroom," Margaret says. "It was, what, forty years ago? And I can still picture it."

"You're getting ahead of me," Kelley says. "I haven't met you yet."

"But you're about to."

"But I'm about to, yes," Kelley says. He sips his wine and cuts into his perfectly cooked roast beef. It's rosy pink, and the Yorkshire pudding is high and light and flecked with chives. He squints at Margaret. "I still don't understand that thing about Martha Stewart."

"What *about* Martha Stewart?" Jen asks.

"Just tell the story, please," Margaret says.

"So, anyway, I was too poor to go home to Perrysburg for Christmas, and my brother, Avery, decided at the last minute to go to Key West with Marcus. Which left me alone in the city. All my roommates went home. We had a sad little wreath on our door, but nobody felt like spending money on a tree. So basically I was looking at a Christmas-less Christmas. I was looking at Chinese takeout and bad TV."

"Sad," Isabelle says.

"It *was* sad. But—never one to feel sorry for myself—I became determined to feel the holiday spirit, and so I took the crosstown bus to the Metropolitan Museum of Art to see the Angel Tree."

Ava nudges Scott. "Ask him what that Angel Tree is."

"What's the Angel Tree, Mr. Quinn?" Scott asks.

Kelley says, "It was a twenty-foot tree on display in one of the galleries that was decorated with angel ornaments. The angels were all different sizes and colors, and they were made from different materials—felt, velvet, metal, straw, wood, cloth, stones, feathers, beads, gold, jewels, you name it—hundreds of different angels on this tree. I got to the museum an hour before it closed on Christmas Eve. Back then, the museum was free with a 'suggested donation' of five dollars. I had five dollars, but I needed to take the crosstown bus home, so I gave the staff member two dollars, but she said since it was late and it was Christmas Eve, I could go in for free."

"Lucky you," Ava says.

"Lucky me," Kelley says. "But not because of the two dollars. I was lucky because the gallery with the tree was empty, and it was dark except for the lights on the tree, and a song was playing. 'Silent Night,' my favorite carol."

"But the gallery wasn't really empty, Daddy, was it?" Ava asks.

"No," Kelley says. "It wasn't."

"It wasn't?" George says. He's leaning forward over his

own loaded dinner plate (he has no problem eating beef, Kelley notices). He's engrossed in the story; next to him, Mitzi sits with her hands in her lap, her sad little dinner untouched. She has heard this story before, right? He must have told her at some point how he and Margaret met, but probably not in this much detail.

"It wasn't empty," Kelley says, "because Margaret was there."

"I was sitting on a bench, staring at the tree," Margaret says. "And Kelley asked if it was okay to sit next to me."

"We didn't speak," Kelley says. "Didn't say a word. We sat and watched the tree and listened to the carols, and then the guard came up and told us the museum was closing. We stood up and walked out together."

"And your father asked me if I wanted to go get hot chocolate," Margaret says. "And I said yes."

"And because I still had five dollars, I had money to pay for it!" Kelley says.

Margaret says, "And that's why, when Ava brought home her paper angel ornament from Sunday school in second grade, it was so special. In fact, I brought it with me last night." She pulls the paper angel out of her pocket like a magician.

"Look at that!" Kelley says. "I remember when Ava made this. I can't believe you still have it!"

"I've had it a long, long time," Margaret says.

"That is a good story," Isabelle says.

There's a clatter at the other end of the table. Mitzi has dropped her knife and fork onto her plate.

"Well," she says, "that was a lovely stroll down memory lane. I'm sure you and Margaret have been scheming about all the possible ways to humiliate me."

"Humiliate *you?*" Kelley says. "That's rich."

"Why is she even *here?*" Mitzi asks. "She hasn't come to Nantucket for Christmas in years. She's too busy and too important to spend the holidays with her own children."

"Watch it," Kelley says.

"I can't believe you're defending her," Mitzi says. "I can't believe you're letting her sit at this table, *in my chair.* I can't believe you let her cook *beef, in my kitchen!*"

"Well," Kelley says, "there are a lot of things I can't believe either. But at least I am adult enough to play through. I am man enough to have invited you and George here for dinner because you had nowhere else to go."

"My suspicions all these years were right," Mitzi says. "You still loved Margaret all the years we were married. You never loved me, and you never cared for Bart."

"Hey, now," Patrick says.

George puts a hand on Mitzi's arm. "Calm down," he says. "You've been drinking."

"Of course I'm DRINKING!" Mitzi screams. "Kelley called up Margaret Quinn, the most famous woman in

America, so the two of them could make me feel like a common whore, when the fact of the matter is, I've been lonely in this marriage for years and years!"

"Mitzi," Kelley says, "please stop. There are children present."

The three kids don't seem interested in Mitzi's soliloquy, however. Pierce is playing with his new iPad under the table.

Jennifer says, "They're finished. Boys, you may be excused."

"Yes," Mitzi says. "I'd like to be excused as well." She stands up and sets the fedora back on her head. "I'm going to the ladies' room."

"Powder room," Kelley says.

Mitzi vanishes.

"Well," Ava says, "I like the story of the Angel Tree."

"So do I," George says. "And, you know, you have a beautiful family. I've always thought that."

"Thank you," Kelley and Margaret say together.

"Does anyone want seconds?" Margaret asks. "Look at all the beef!"

"Sandwiches tomorrow," Kevin says.

Kelley eats dinner, trying to savor it. Maybe it *was* insensitive to tell the Angel Tree story? Okay, yes, it was, but he didn't tell it to ruin Mitzi's night. Okay, maybe he *did* tell it to ruin Mitzi's night, but doesn't she deserve it? A little bit?

The food is *so delicious,* he can't believe it. He wonders if Margaret made dessert. He noticed that Mrs. Gabler brought a plum pudding. Would Margaret be able to whip up some of her hard sauce to go with it?

His vision of sugar plums is interrupted by Mitzi, who storms back into the dining room. Her face is as red as her hat. She is holding something up in her hand, something shiny. She is shaking it.

"Look what I found next to your bed!" she shouts.

Kelley opens his mouth to protest. Did he or did he not tell her to use the *powder room?* But did she listen? No. No, she marched right into the master suite. Possibly she was after the remaining inch of her organic hairspray. She doesn't like to waste *anything,* and she might have worried that Kelley wouldn't recycle the bottle properly.

Margaret gasps. Under the table, her hand grabs Kelley's knee.

Kelley squints to focus on what Mitzi is holding in her hand.

"Margaret's watch," Mitzi says, "was on your bedside table."

Everyone at the table is rendered silent.

Margaret says, "I'll take that now, Mitzi, please. I didn't realize I left it there."

"You must have taken it off before you slept with my husband."

"Mitzi...," George says.

"That hideous watch!" Mitzi says, rattling it like a castanet. "I see you wearing it on the news. It ruins your already ugly outfits."

233

"Mitzi!" Ava cries out. "Honestly! You sound like you're ten years old."

"Wait a minute," Margaret says, "are *you* the one who writes the blog about me? Are you Queenie229?"

"I hate this watch because I know who gave it to you," Mitzi says.

"*I* gave it to her," Kelley says.

"Yes," Margaret says, "after Ava was born. That was long before he met you, Mitzi; there's no reason for you to feel threatened."

"Except that you wear it every single night on the *national news* as a signal that you still love him! It's always sickened me! And it further sickens me that you showed up here and crawled right into bed with Kelley only a scant day after I crawled out!"

At this, both Patrick and Kevin stand up to defend their mother's honor, but Margaret is hung up on something different.

"*Are you* Queenie229?" she asks Mitzi.

Yes, Kelley thinks. "Queenie" for Roller Disco Queen of King of Prussia, PA, and 2/29 is Mitzi's birthday. Leap Day.

Mitzi says, "Not everyone in America loves you. Not everyone in America thinks you have impeccable style."

"Well, I'm glad I know it's you," Margaret says. "Although trashing your husband's ex-wife anonymously in a blog is a move I would have thought was beneath you. It's tasteless."

"That's it!" Mitzi says. "I've had it. I'm not going to stay here while you insult me. George, we're leaving."

George stuffs a large piece of roast beef into his mouth and takes one more snowflake roll before he stands up. "Yes, dear," he says weakly. It sounds like he and Mitzi have been married fifty years.

Kelley pulls out the present from Mitzi and quickly opens it. It's a Barefoot Contessa cookbook; Mitzi gives him the newest one every year.

"Thank you for this," he says. He holds the book up like a librarian at story time, showing everyone the cover.

"Oh," Margaret says, "I love the Barefoot Contessa, and I know her. Ina Garten. I can introduce you, if you like."

"I'll tell you what's *shameless,*" Mitzi says. "Your name-dropping is shameless!"

"I for one would love to meet the Barefoot Contessa," Isabelle says.

"You!" Mitzi says. "I saved you, Isabelle. You would have been sent home long ago if it weren't for me. But you have taken her side, too."

"It isn't about sides," Ava says. "She's our mother."

"And you *were* our stepmother," Kevin says.

"Merry Christmas, Mitzi, George. Good night," Kelley says. He does not stand up, however. He is going to sit and finish what's on his plate, and he may even have seconds.

Mitzi and George leave the dining room, but Kelley waits until the front door slams shut before he resumes eating. He meant to tell Mitzi that Eddie Pancik will be listing the inn, but that can wait until after the holidays.

He smiles at Margaret. "What are you doing on New Year's?"

"I'm broadcasting from Times Square," she says. "Wanna come?"

AVA

She and Scott offer to do the dishes between dinner and dessert. Everyone else tops off their glasses and heads out to sit by the fire.

"I never really understood the term 'family circus,'" Ava says, "until the past two days."

"I like your family," Scott says.

"You're insane," Ava says.

"Yeah," Scott says. "I know."

But actually, Scott is the sanest person Ava knows. And, in addition to having superhero shoulders, he has the biggest, sweetest heart. She remembers when Scott came into her classroom as she was trying to teach twenty-two fourth graders how to play "Annie's Song" on the recorder. It was cacophony, to say the least. Scott interrupted the class, pulling Ava aside to tell her that Claire Frye's mother had been killed. Ava had stared at Scott in horror, willing herself not to cry. He squeezed her hand and said calmly, "I'm going to bring Claire to the office now. Her father is waiting."

Ava watched Scott lead Claire from the classroom, his hand lightly on her back, his posture ramrod straight, his eyes showing nothing but kindness and some man-of-steel internal strength.

Later that day, Ava swung by Scott's office. He was at his desk, holding his head in his hands. He didn't move when Ava came in, and for a while she watched him, wondering if he'd had to witness the moment when Claire Frye learned her mother was dead.

Scott said, "God, I hope I never have to do anything like that ever, ever again."

Only now does Ava remember how she had, in that moment, loved him with every cell in her body.

Now there is the other thing eating at her, the new sexual energy between them. The magnetic attraction. She still doesn't understand how it just appeared out of nowhere. She held Scott's hand under the table through a good part of dinner, and even the hand-holding was a turn-on.

She says, "I broke up with Nathaniel."

"You did not."

"I did. I called him and ended it."

Scott swallows. "Not...because of me?"

"Not because of you, no. Because of me. I'm sick and tired of chasing after something that's never going to happen."

Scott nods once; she can see him trying to understand. "But you still have feelings for him."

"Yes," Ava says. "But that doesn't matter. I'm finished."

"Really?" Scott says.

"Really," Ava says. She gives Scott's tie a tug, and before she knows it, she and Scott are kissing up against the sink, next to the half-loaded dishwasher, and the water is running.

She stops him. "Let's finish here," she says, "and go to my bedroom."

"Okay," he says, breathless.

The dishes get done very, very quickly after that.

Ava leads Scott down the hallway, to her bedroom. She lies on the bed and pulls Scott on top of her. They make out like teenagers for what feels like an hour. Out in the main room, Ava hears her mother announce that dessert is ready— plum pudding with hard sauce. Ava *loves* plum pudding with hard sauce, and she knows her father will be making his famous Irish coffees—but nothing in the world right now is sweeter than being with Scott.

As he runs his hand up her sweater, her phone rings. She catches the display out of the corner of her eye. *NO,* it says.

Nathaniel.

Scott says, "Do you have to answer that?"

"No," she says.

Ava stops Scott somewhere between second and third base. It's not that she doesn't want to keep going; it's that she wants something to look forward to.

"Okay, right," Scott says. He sounds like he's trying to convince himself. "It will be better if we wait."

"Just not too long," she says.

After a while she tiptoes to the kitchen to snag two dishes of plum pudding for herself and Scott—she hopes there is some left—and she overhears her parents in the kitchen, talking.

Margaret says, "You don't have to sell the inn. I could either lend you the money to keep it going, or I could buy it outright and you could run it."

"Kevin wants to run it," Kelley says. "Kevin and Isabelle."

"Do they?" Margaret says. "Would that be a bad life for them?"

"I can't let you buy the inn, Maggie," Kelley says. "You've already done too much as it is."

"What have I done?" Margaret asks. "I showed up, is all. And I was long overdue for that."

Ava strolls into the kitchen. "Hello, parents," she says. "So, are you two getting back together, or what?"

They both laugh. Ava gets two dishes of plum pudding and douses them with her mother's luscious hard sauce. She asks Kelley to make two Irish coffees.

"This may come as a shock," Ava says, "but since we're all being honest, I'm entertaining a guest in my room."

"Scott is lovely," Margaret says.

"We just want you to be happy, sweetheart," Kelley says.

Ava takes dessert back to her room on a tray, thinking, *Sell the inn?* Well, it's time, probably, that she found her own place to live.

But still...sell the inn?

She and Scott gobble down dessert, and then they turn on the TV to watch *It's a Wonderful Life* while drinking their Irish coffee.

Then they must have both fallen asleep, because Ava wakes up to someone knocking on her bedroom door.

"Ava!" It's her mother. "Ava, are you in there?"

Ava stands up, collects herself, and opens the door. "Hi, what is it?"

Her mother mouths something, but Ava is too bleary-eyed to make out what it is.

"What?"

Margaret leans in and whispers, "Nathaniel is here."

Ava blinks. "Here?"

Her mother nods vigorously.

Nathaniel is here.

Ava turns to look at Scott. He is passed out cold in her bed. Ava tiptoes out into the hallway, closing the door gently behind her.

*   *   *

Nathaniel is in the living room, chitchatting with Kevin, listening to Kevin and Isabelle's big news, admiring Isabelle's diamond ring.

"Wow, that's great!" Nathaniel says. "I'm really psyched for you guys."

"Thanks," Kevin says.

Nathaniel sees Ava and breaks into that heart-stopping grin of his, the same one he gave her the day he met her.

"Hey, baby," he says.

She will not succumb.

She says, "Let's go to the kitchen."

"Or your room?" he says.

"No."

"Wow," he says. "You really are mad."

She strides into the kitchen but finds Kelley in there, cleaning up dessert and making fresh muffins for the morning.

"Hey, Ava," he says. Funny look. "Hey, Nathaniel."

"Mr. Quinn," Nathaniel says. "Merry Christmas."

"And to you," Kelley says.

Ava can't believe it is *still* Christmas. This is the Christmas that never ends.

She says, "Well, we can't talk in the kitchen, so we'll have to talk in the dining room."

"Or your room," he says.

"No," Ava says.

"Or we can go to my place," Nathaniel says.

"Negative," Ava says.

"Wow," Nathaniel says. "Where did you get that necklace? Did *Scott* give you that necklace?"

"None of your business," Ava says.

"Did Scott give you the necklace, Ava? If he did, then this makes sense. I mean, one guy gives you rain boots, one guy gives you a diamond necklace..."

Ava sighs. "It's from my mother."

"Oh," Nathaniel says.

"Let me be clear," Ava says. "I'm not *mad*. I'm just finished."

"You don't love me?" he says.

"Whether or not I love you doesn't matter," Ava says. "It's over. I'm tired of waiting around for you to treat me the way I want to be treated. Love me the way I want to be loved."

"You want *what*, exactly?" Nathaniel says. "You want me to get down on one knee and propose? Fine, I will." He sinks to the ground. "Ava Quinn, will you marry me?"

"You don't mean it," Ava says.

"I do so," he says. "I love you. I am probably guilty of taking you for granted, but the flip side is that loving you is so easy. Being with you is comfortable. You're normal and cool, there isn't any drama, you don't ask me for things, you let me be me. When I went to Seattle this fall, you didn't bat an eye, you didn't complain or call me selfish—and I *was* being selfish, and I was a jackass for not inviting you along, but I needed to get away, *alone,* and you got it. You get *me.* I love you, Ava. Now, will you marry me?"

Ava feels like she's breaking in half. Nathaniel is saying all the right things, and it is true that she loves him. But something isn't right. She doesn't want to be comfortable, like a sweater or a dish of vanilla pudding. She wants something better than that.

"Ava," Nathaniel says. "Please. I want you to be my wife."

Ava teeters. She wobbles. This is her heart's one desire for Christmas coming true. Coming true after all.

Suddenly, Scott appears in the doorway of the dining room. His hair is mussed, and his tie hangs loose. Ava thinks of how he came rushing out of the parking lot without a winter coat just to check on her. How he stopped by the Bar to take her home. How he looks at her and she feels like she is the most beautiful, desirable woman in the universe.

"No," she says to Nathaniel.

"Oh, baby, come on!" Nathaniel says.

"No," she says. "Now get up, please."

"Ava," he says, "I know you want this."

"I don't," she says. "Please stand up."

"Nathaniel," Scott says, suddenly sounding like Assistant Principal Skyler, "stand up."

Nathaniel's head swivels around. He sees Scott, and recognition comes into his eyes. He gets to his feet.

"I'll walk you to the door," Scott says.

MARGARET

Kevin and Isabelle go to bed first. Isabelle looks utterly exhausted, the kind of exhausted only known to pregnant women in their first trimester. She kisses Margaret on both cheeks and thanks her for the wonderful dinner. It's the first meal she's managed to keep down in weeks, she says.

"I'll take that as a sign that my future grandchild likes my cooking," Margaret says.

Jennifer takes the kids upstairs to one of the rooms at the inn and puts them to bed. Patrick follows behind her, but first he stops to give Margaret a long hug.

"I'll give you Hollis Chambers's number in the morning," Margaret says. "I've always got your back."

"I know you do, Mom," he says.

"You're my golden boy," she says.

"But not anymore," he says.

"Oh, honey," she says. "Yes, you are. Forever you are."

Nathaniel leaves, and then a little while later, Scott bids everyone good-bye.

Margaret says to Ava, "Are you okay, honey?"

Ava sits down at the piano and starts to play "While Shepherds Watched Their Flocks by Night," very softly. The fire crackles, the tree shimmers. Kelley is laid out lengthwise on the sofa, his feet in Margaret's lap. She thinks she sees snowflakes out the window. It would be a nice way to end Christmas, with a light, pretty snowfall. Maybe Margaret can take the kids sledding tomorrow.

She stands up and goes over to the window to check.

Yes, snow!

Ava says, "This one is for you, Daddy." She starts to play "Silent Night."

Silent night, holy night, all is calm, all is bright

Margaret sings into the cold window; her breath fogs up the pane.

Round yon virgin mother and child, holy infant so
 tender and mild

Kelley says to Margaret, "So, Maggie, how long do you think you'll stay?"

Margaret pulls the paper angel out of her pocket and presses it to her chest. This time with Kelley has been magical. She has spent the last twenty-four hours in a state of delirious happiness, and they brought closure to certain issues—they are the best of friends, and they will always love each other. Who knows, they may even decide to be buried together. But when Margaret replays Ava's question, *So, are you two getting back together, or what?*—Margaret thinks, *No. It will never work out.* The same thing will happen. Margaret will become absorbed in her work, and Kelley will resent it.

Sleep in heavenly peace, sleep in heavenly peace.

Margaret's phone buzzes, which startles her. She hasn't had a text all day except for the marriage proposal from Drake.

Would it be so bad to marry a surgeon? she wonders.

She checks her phone. The text is from Darcy. It says: *Bart Quinn was on that convoy. He and the 44 other soldiers have been officially announced missing. I'm so sorry. You may already know this. Family is being notified presently.*

Margaret stifles a cry just as a phone rings in the house.

Kelley says, "That's weird. No one ever calls the landline. Maybe it's Eddie Pancik with a buyer." He stands up.

No. Nonononono! Margaret thinks. *Not on Christmas!* Missing, not dead. But still…missing. *Missing!*

Tears blur Margaret's eyes, but she doesn't want Kelley's peace of mind shattered one second sooner than it needs to be. She intercepts him on his way to answer the phone. She gives him a kiss on the lips and looks straight into his blue eyes.

"I'll stay as long as you need me to," she says.

ACKNOWLEDGMENTS

I'd like to thank my family, present and past.

My siblings: Eric Hilderbrand, Randall Osteen, Heather Osteen Thorpe, Douglas Hilderbrand. Also Lisa Hilderbrand and Todd Thorpe, Doug and Katharine Thurman, and Debra Thurman.

The gang: Robert, Patrick, Alexandra, Garrett, Parker, Spence, Tripp, and Anna.

My mother, Sally Hilderbrand, who is the undisputed Ornament Queen of Christmas, and my nutcracker go-to.

Judith and Duane Thurman, who have been like parents to me, and brought the Byers' Choice carolers into my life.

Frank and Sue Cunningham, thank you for the Golden Dreams.

My grandparents: Bob and Bobbie Hilderbrand, and Clarence and Ruth Huling.

My aunts and uncles: Jan and Ruthann Hall, and Steve

and Ruth Huling, and Alice; Jane Greene and my cousins Debi and Wendy.

My elves, the stars on my trees, my (not always) angels: Maxwell, Dawson, and Shelby.

My last best Christmas was the Christmas of 1983. My father and Judy and my siblings and I went to Mass at St. David's Episcopal, where there was a live menagerie and a choir of angels, the church at five p.m. lit only by candles. On the way home, we stopped by a friend's house to drink hot chocolate made with milk, vanilla, and cinnamon, and admire their twenty-foot Christmas tree. Then we headed home to watch Michael Jackson's new video "Thriller," for the first time. We ordered pizza and cheesesteaks, wrote our letters to Santa, and crawled into bed. It was the last Christmas I spent at my father's house while he was alive, and so the memories are burnished not because of the details above, but because he was the one who tucked us in.

Christmas is about people. And I am grateful for those who are, and have been, in my life, but especially for my father, Robert H. Hilderbrand Jr.

BACK BAY · READERS' PICK

Reading Group Guide

WINTER STREET

A NOVEL

by

Elin Hilderbrand

An online version of this reading group guide is available at littlebrown.com.

A conversation with
Elin Hilderbrand

What are your favorite and least favorite Christmas carols?

My favorite carols are "O Holy Night," "O Come, All Ye Faithful," and "The First Noel." My least favorite carol is "Jingle Bells." I just despise it. That may seem like blasphemy, but—like Ava—I far prefer carols with substance.

What are your favorite holiday traditions?

My favorite tradition as an adult has been making Christmas baskets for my kids' teachers and certain of my friends. Unlike most people who give cookies or sweets, I started making "savory baskets" that include corn muffins with flavored butters, summer sausage with homemade mustard, potato chips with homemade chive pine-nut dip, cheddar tartlets, and macadamia butter-crunch popcorn. I figure that my friends can set out these goodies as appetizers before their big holiday meals, or they can serve them if they have unexpected guests stop by.

What are your fondest Christmas memories?

My fondest memories are from ages ten to thirteen when I was still a child but old enough to appreciate the beauty and the meaning of the holiday. My father died when I was sixteen, so I only had fifteen Christmases with him, and those last few are the ones that meant the most.

What are the best and worst Christmas gifts you've ever received?

There was one year where I received both a vacuum cleaner and a dictionary. I'll leave it at that.

Have you ever spent the holidays away from home or those you love?

In 1994, I spent Christmas on the beach in Thailand, when I was traveling through Southeast Asia for six months. I think I took it pretty hard—I was enjoying the tropical beach, but I missed my family, so much so that my clearest memory of that day was standing in line at the communications office waiting for an international phone line with all of the Australians. More recently, I spent Christmas on the Big Island in Hawaii, and I have to say, it was pretty nice to wake up and head to the beach and then have someone else cook me a big fat Christmas dinner.

I think that as I've grown older and my siblings and I have had our own families and started our own traditions that it inevitably turns out that I am missing someone. That's why the memories of being a young adolescent stand out as my best Christmases—because everyone who was important to me at that time was there. As I say in my acknowledgments, Christmas is about people, and I am happy now if I can spend the holidays with even some of the people I hold dear.

What are your favorite stories to tell around the Christmas dinner table?

I grew up in a blended family of five children, and the stories we like to tell are about the gifts we gave one another in college, none of which are appropriate to repeat in these pages. My sister, Heather, was notorious for speaking very quickly, and one year my brothers bought her a special tape recorder that slowed her words down so we could all understand them. We all cracked up at that.

What holiday decorations would your Christmas not be complete without?

It may come as no surprise that my most treasured decorations are my mother's collection of nutcrackers (she has as many as Mitzi) and a paper angel that I made when I was in the third grade. My mother also makes an ornament every year, which she gives each child and grandchild, so my entire tree is decorated with Sally Hilderbrand ornaments — except for glass balls, which always go on the inside of the branches so that it looks like the tree is glowing from within.

What makes the holidays stressful?

In general, I feel expectations are too high during the holidays. My philosophy is to keep things low-key and pick a few areas that are going to be my focus. I buy great presents, and I cook a great roast. I get good seats for Christmas Eve Mass, and I enjoy the luxury of caviar with my best friends. Other than that, I let things unfold as they may. Merry Christmas! Happy New Year!

Questions and topics for discussion

1. Ava has a passionate dislike of "Jingle Bells." What are your favorite and least favorite Christmas carols? Why?

2. When Margaret tries to remember the last time Christmas meant something really special to her besides a much-needed vacation, she harkens back to a vivid memory of a Christmas morning when Patrick and Kevin were in middle school and Ava was five years old. What are your fondest memories of Christmas morning?

3. The Quinn family Christmas celebration is full of special traditions—including cooking a standing rib roast, Golden Dream cocktails, and an appearance by Santa Claus. What are your favorite holiday traditions? What special meanings do they hold for you?

4. Before changing her holiday travel plans to visit Kelley and her children in Nantucket, Margaret was planning to travel to Hawaii for Christmas. Have you ever spent Christmas in a tropical destination? If so, how did it affect your holiday experience?

5. Every family has holiday decorations that they hold dear. For Mitzi, it's her nutcrackers and caroler figurines, while for Margaret it's the paper angel ornament that Ava made when she was in second grade. What decorations are a treasured part of your family's holiday celebrations? What memories are associated with them?

6. Bart's absence during the Christmas festivities weighs heavily on all the Quinns. Have you ever had to spend Christmas apart from those you love the most?

7. Kelley recounts the story of how he met Margaret, a story that he used to tell every Christmas during the Quinn family Christmas dinner. Are there any familiar stories that are told every year during your family's holiday celebrations?

8. Ava is disappointed with the gift of rain boots and matching socks that she receives from her boyfriend, Nathaniel. Have you ever received a disappointing gift from a significant other that clarified how you felt about them?

9. As we see in *Winter Street,* holiday celebrations can turn into a "family circus" even though the family members love one another immensely. What is it about the holidays that can bring family tensions to the forefront despite the peaceful, loving mood of the season?

ABOUT THE AUTHOR

Elin Hilderbrand made a paper angel ornament in third grade that is still in her family's custody. She celebrates the holidays by making batches of mustard and chive pine-nut dip and gifting them to her friends. Her favorite carol is "O Holy Night." *Winter Street* is her fourteenth novel.

...AND HER NEXT CHRISTMAS NOVEL

In *Winter Stroll,* the Quinn family celebrates their most dramatic Christmas yet. Following is an excerpt from the novel's opening pages.

Friday, December 4

MITZI

She sneaks out behind the hotel and lights a cigarette. George knows she smokes, but he has drawn the line at watching her do it—so she has to be stealthy and quick. If she's gone for more than ten minutes he sends out a search party, which is usually comprised of himself and his Jack Russell terrier, Rudy, but also sometimes one or more of the women who work in the shop making hats. George thinks Mitzi is going to hurt herself. Or, possibly, run off and have an affair on him, the way she did on her husband, Kelley.

An affair is unthinkable in Mitzi's condition. Hurting herself seems redundant; she is already suffering from the maximum amount of pain a person can experience.

Bart Bart Bart Bart Bart.

George says he understands, but he's never had a child, so how could he possibly?

Nicotine is poison. And yet, since Bart has gone missing, cigarettes are one of two things that make Mitzi feel better. The other is alcohol. Mitzi has become partial to a sipping tequila called Casa Dragones that is packaged in a slender, elegant turquoise box and costs eighty-five dollars a bottle at the one high-end liquor store in Lenox that sells it.

She wonders if any of the liquor stores on Nantucket sell Casa Dragones. Murray's, perhaps? She would like a few shots of it now, just enough to take the edge off.

When Bart enlisted in the Marines eighteen months earlier, Mitzi had naively believed the so-called War Against Terror to be *over*. Osama bin Laden had been killed and buried at sea. Mitzi had pictured Bart going to Afghanistan to help a war-torn people get back on their feet. She had thought he would be digging wells and rebuilding schools. She had envisioned him working with children—giving them pencils and gum, teaching them inappropriate phrases in English. *Baby got back!* But Bart had been in country less than twenty-four hours when his convoy of forty-five troops was captured.

They have been missing for nearly a year now.

The Department of Defense believes that the extremist group responsible for the kidnapping is called the *Bely,* pronounced "belle-aye." It means "yes" in the Afghan language. No one has ever heard of the Bely; all that is known about them is that they are young—most of them only teenagers— and they are vicious. One official reportedly said, "These kids make ISIS and the Taliban look like Up with People." The Bely are also, apparently, magicians—because even after sending three reconnaissance missions into Sangin and the surrounding province, the U.S. military has yet to discover where the marines are being held.

Mitzi can't watch TV anymore, nor read the newspaper; she can barely log on to her computer. When there is *definitive news* about what has happened to Bart's convoy, the DoD will contact Kelley and Mitzi directly.

George's advice is: *Try not to think about it.* This is apparently how they deal with misfortune at the North Pole. They ignore it.

Mitzi finishes her cigarette, stubs it out on the sole of her clog, and pops a breath mint—for what reason, she's not quite sure. George doesn't kiss her anymore, and they rarely have sex. George is older and requires the help of a pill to be intimate, and Mitzi can't lose herself for even half an hour. She is a prisoner as well—to her worry, her fear, her anxiety, and her bad habits.

She pulls out her cell phone and calls Kelley.

"Hello?" he says. His voice sounds robust, nearly happy; in the background, Mitzi can hear Christmas music, "Carol of the Bells." Mitzi has many issues with Kelley, but chief among them is how, at times, he doesn't even seem to remember that their son is missing. He has handled Bart's disappearance with an equanimity Mitzi finds baffling. Case in point: right now, he seems to be listening to carols! And he's probably getting ready to make champagne cocktails for the guests. It's Christmas Stroll weekend—which, on Nantucket, is even more Christmassy than Christmas itself. The town has an intoxicating smell of evergreen, salt air, and woodsmoke. When the ferry rounded Brant Point earlier that afternoon and Mitzi saw the giant lit wreath hanging on the lighthouse, she remembered, for an instant, just how much she loved the holidays on this island.

But then, reality descended like a dark hood.

"Kelley," Mitzi says. "I'm here."

"Here?" Kelley says.

"On Nantucket," she says. "For the weekend. We're staying at the Castle."

"For the love of all Harry, Mitzi," Kelley says. "Why?"

Why? Why? Why? She and Kelley had agreed that it would be best for everyone if Mitzi stayed with George in Lenox through the holidays.

"You made your decision," Kelley had said, on the other occasions when Mitzi had mentioned returning to Nantucket for a visit. "You chose George."

I chose George, Mitzi thought. For twelve years running, Mitzi and George had conducted a love affair during the Christmas holidays, when George brought his antique fire engine to the island and dressed up as the Winter Street Inn Santa Claus. Last year, things had come to a head, and Mitzi had decided to leave Kelley for George. Bart had *just* deployed and Mitzi's judgment had been wobbly. More than

5

anything, she had wanted to escape her circumstances; she had wanted to hide in a fantasy life of sleigh bells and elves.

It had been a big fat mistake. Now that Mitzi is with George day in, day out, the allure has worn thin. Who wants to be with Santa Claus on St. Patrick's Day, or the Fourth of July? Nobody. Santa's sex appeal is specific to the month of December. On good days, Mitzi feels a brotherly affection for George; on bad days, she is filled with bitter regret.

"I had to come," Mitzi says. "I missed the island so much, and I know Kevin and Isabelle are having the baby baptized on Sunday."

"How?" Kelley says. "How did you know that?"

Mitzi crunches her breath mint. She doesn't want to give away her source.

"Ava certainly didn't tell you," Kelley says. "And it wasn't Kevin or Isabelle. And Patrick is in jail."

Another second and he'll figure it out, Mitzi thinks.

"Jennifer!" Kelley says. "Jennifer told you. I can't believe she still speaks to you. She actually *is* the nicest person alive, just as we always suspected."

"Jennifer and I are simpatico," Mitzi says. "She lost her husband, and I lost my son."

"She did not *lose* her husband," Kelley says. "Patrick is in jail, he's not *dead*. And"—here Kelley clears his throat—"Bart isn't dead, either, Mitzi."

Mitzi squeezes her eyes shut. She can't explain how badly she needs to hear Kelley say that. *Bart isn't dead*. Which means, Bart is alive. He's somewhere. The Bely are a new enemy, but the one thing that is known about them is their tender age. The only way Mitzi gets through some nights is to imagine Bart and the other marines playing soccer or gin rummy with their counterparts in the Bely.

When Mitzi shared this vision with George, he gave her an encouraging pat and said, "That's the ticket, Mrs. Claus."

Mitzi has become pen pals with the mothers of two of the other missing marines through a service provided by the Department of Defense, and although they are from vastly different backgrounds—one woman is a fundamentalist Christian in Tallahassee, Florida, and one woman lives on Flatbush Avenue in Brooklyn, both women are black—the emails sustain Mitzi and provide her with a sense of community. There are at least two other people in the world who understand exactly what Mitzi is feeling.

"Can I come to the baptism?" Mitzi asks. "Please?"

There is a great big huff from Kelley. "I really want to tell you 'no,'" he says. "You left *me,* you cheated on *me,* you betrayed *me,* you broke *my* heart, Mitzi."

"I know," she says. "I'm sorry."

"If it was just the one time, I might have understood," Kelley says. "But twelve years? It was a willful, planned, long-standing deceit, Mitzi."

"I know," Mitzi says. They have been over this same ground dozens and dozens of times in the past year, and

Mitzi finds the best strategy is to agree with Kelley rather than try to defend herself.

" 'Peace on earth, good will toward men,' Luke chapter 2, the Annunciation to the shepherds," Kelley says. "Because that is my Christmas mantra this year, I'm going to concede. You can come to the baptism. It's at eleven o'clock on Sunday. I'll save two seats in our pew for you and George."

"Thank you," Mitzi says. She would have gone to the baptism even without Kelley's permission, but it feels better to have asked. And two seats in the family pew is more than she dreamed of.

"You're welcome," Kelley says. "Forget what I said about Jennifer. *I'm* the nicest person alive."

Mitzi hangs up the phone just as George steps out the back door of the hotel.

"I've been looking all over for you," he says. He waves two tickets in the air. "Are you ready for the Holiday House Tour?"

Bart Bart Bart Bart Bart. Mitzi always says his name five times in her mind, like a prayer.